OAKTOWN DEVIL

OAKTOWN DEVIL

RENAY JACKSON

Frog, Ltd.
Berkeley, California

Published by Frog, Ltd.

Frog, Ltd. books are distributed by
North Atlantic Books
P.O. Box 12327
Berkeley, California 94712

Cover illustrations © 2004 Ariel Shepard
Cover and book design by Maxine Ressler

Printed in the United States of America

Distributed to the book trade by Publishers Group West

North Atlantic Books' publications are available through most bookstores. For further information, call 800-337-2665 or visit our website at www.northatlanticbooks.com.

Substantial discounts on bulk quantities are available to corporations, professional associations, and other organizations. For details and discount information, contact our special sales department.

Library of Congress Cataloging-in-Publication Data

Jackson, Renay, 1959–
Oaktown devil / by Renay Jackson.
p. cm.
ISBN 1-58394-105-3 (pbk.)
1. Murder victims' families — Fiction. 2. Brothers — Death — Fiction.
3. Drug traffic — Fiction. I. Title.
PS3610.A3547O15 2004
813'.6 — dc22

2004007143

1 2 3 4 5 6 7 8 9 DATA 09 08 07 06 05 04

A narrow mind
and wide mouth
usually go together.

—*anonymous*

Nothing beats a failure
but a try.

—*anonymous*

Dedicated to PJ, Resa, Pookie, and Vasaty,
"my driving influence."

To my mom Patricia:
"Mama, excuse the language."

. . .

The sound of running water . . .
. . . makes me wanna pee.
—a janitor's wisdom

Author's Note

This book is based totally on the writer's imagination. Any similarities to actual events are purely coincidental. Although many of the locations are real, they were used only to make the story believable.

SHOUTS

APRYL JEAN LADAY — HONEY, WITHOUT
YOU HANDLING EVERYTHING I DON'T, WE
COULD NOT PROSPER. THANK YOU.

IRMA LEWIS — GURLL, YOU'VE
ALWAYS BEEN IN MY CORNER, AND IT'S
TRULY APPRECIATED.

PATRICIA TURNER — MOMMA,
NO AMOUNT OF WORDS CAN POSSIBLY
DESCRIBE THE LOVE I HAVE FOR YOU.

FRIENDS OF CHESTER HIMES —
YOU GUYS HAVE HELPED MY CAREER SO
MUCH THAT I WILL ALWAYS BE GRATEFUL.

MY DAUGHTERS AND NIECES — MY MOST
VOCAL SUPPORTERS.

THE LORD ALMIGHTY — NEED I SAY MORE?

TABLE OF CONTENTS

1
THE GIRL OF MY DREAMS

It was a very hot summer day, at least ninety-five degrees. So hot you could see waves in front of your eyes. After procrastinating all morning I finally washed the car. By the time I was done my mouth was so dry I knew if I didn't hurry up and quench my thirst, I'd probably pass out. Jumping in the Accord, I headed to Baskin-Robbins for a smoothie. That was when I noticed her. She needed directions, I supplied the information. During our brief conversation we realized that we shared many things in common. Things like cooking, bar-b-que, reading, jazz, and computers. She wore blue painted-on Levi 501s, matching blue sneakers, and a light blue tank top. The girl was phine. After the usual rap about where you work, school you went to, what you do on weekends (along with elevator-eyeing each other), we exchanged phone numbers. Her name was Cassandra.

Our phone conversations were cool. We would talk for hours but it only seemed like minutes. She was a divorced mother of two struggling from check to check. Her job with the government paid well and she also received sporadic child support, but Cassandra still found her cash flow to be a bit short. "Twenty-nine years old and stuck in neutral" is how she put it.

We agreed to go out on a date. The plan was for me to pick her up at seven-thirty Wednesday evening, but she had to be home by midnight. This was reasonable, since we both had jobs to report to the next day. I spent all of Wednesday making plans. I wanted this to be a night she would always remember. Based on our conversations, it was obvious she hadn't been out in a long time. I put my game plan in effect.

I got to Cassandra's place at seven-fifteen. She lived in a four-plex painted blue with white trim, located in East Oaktown near the mall. Each unit had a private garage, balcony, and washer/dryer hookup. There were flowerbeds off to the side of each door. Considering the area, this was a very nice and quiet block. I walked up to her door and rang the bell.

I had on a blue Italian designer suit, sky-blue shirt with a white collar that had two holes from which I wore a gold bar and looping chain, blue suede Stacy Adams, and powder-blue "pimp" socks. On my left hand was a huge gold nugget ring with a matching nugget watch on my arm. My right hand sported a gold cluster ring with eight tiny diamonds surrounding one huge stone. On my right arm was a nugget bracelet purchased for twenty dollars from a neighborhood dope fiend. With horned-rimmed glasses, stud earring, fresh cut and trim, necktie with all the colors under the sun, and Aramis cologne, I was fitted to a tee, and her expression when Cassandra opened the door told me that she was impressed.

Pulling my arm out from behind my back, I handed her the dozen roses I'd bought from a nice downtown florist. There were four pink, four white, and four red blooms, complete with baby's breath and all the trimmings. The glass vase was something I found under my kitchen cabinet and cleaned to a sparkle. This temporarily caught her off guard because she pulled me into her arms and gave me a very passionate kiss. Apologizing while backing away, she mumbled something about having to finish getting dressed and disappeared to her bedroom. My hormones raced wildly. I was ready to forget about going out and just spend the night romancing here like mad. Anyway, I regained my composure and waited patiently while she struggled to regain hers.

I glanced around her living room. It was obvious the girl had taste. She had a matching black leather sofa and loveseat that were plush. The antique wooden coffee table had a flowerpot in the center with a cool floral arrangement; it was placed over a Persian rug. In the corner sat a Sony component set complete with surround sound, CD, dual cassettes, tuner, receiver, and six speakers of various sizes carefully placed around the room. I had recently priced one of these units for fifteen C-notes, so I knew she had style. Her CD collection was ample, with Luther belting out "Love Don't Love You Anymore." On her wall above the music center were three picture frames which held six shots each. They were photos taken of her family at various affairs. Her twenty-five-inch floor-model boob tube came complete with swivel action. On top was a VCR, along with 8x10" framed pictures of her children.

Directly above the TV on the wall hung a very large picture. It was the centerpiece of the room, what I like to call the focal point. On it was a cougar walking through bushes with a full moon radiating above. The backdrop was blue and black with gold trim. On each side were three mirror strips. This entire picture was framed in black, and the whole thing was a mirror. It wasn't the most expensive item in the house, but to me it represented class.

With black vertical blinds, black dinette set with leather chairs that matched the couch, black custom-made work station in the corner holding an IBM 386 clone, and assorted plants throughout, Cassandra's home was tastefully decorated. Her finishing touch was an entire wall behind the sofa covered with those little mirror squares that you stick on, illuminated by a floor-to-ceiling drooping lamp (yes, in black).

Finally, Cassandra reappeared and the girl was stunning. A blue strapless dress hugged every curve, and curves she had. It came down to mid thigh and showed off her athletically built legs, which were greased and shiny from baby oil. She wore blue Brazilian shoes and no stockings. This only enhanced the effect her legs had on me. She had rings on every finger except the thumbs, bangle bracelets on the right arm, gold watch on the left, and toted what I call a party purse, which is one of those tiny things that appear to have only enough room for makeup, money and ID, but always seem to contain everything a woman needs. The purse, also blue, was in perfect taste.

On her neck were two shiny gold necklaces. One had a cross and the other spelled out "Dad." Cassandra wore black lipstick, which looked very nice on her midnight-black skin. Her earrings were those big loops that people wore with afros back in the seventies, and her hair was done in braids. She'd previously told me that she always got her hair done at Sherry's on MacArthur Boulevard, and I couldn't help wondering how much of the shoulder-length stuff was hers, and how much came from the beauty supply store.

"Okay, let's go," she said with anticipation.

As she went to turn off the TV, her lovely heart-shaped behind switched with every move. It looked as though you could balance a glass on top and it would not fall off. I knew then that I would be the envy of every man in the club tonight. Taking Cassandra by the hand, I closed the door and we left.

"You have a very nice car," she said.

"Thank you," I replied.

As she slid into the passenger side of "Bertha," her dress hiked up extremely high, revealing meat you would die for. I tried not to let her notice that my wandering eyes were zooming in on her assets, so I walked to the other side, opened my door, and attempted to casually slide in.

My hooptie was the bomb that night. Earlier I had it washed and waxed at the spot on 38th & Foothill. They did their usual fine job hooking up the tires with the wet look, spraying the carpet with a sweet-smelling strawberry fragrance, and polishing the dash, steering wheel, seats, panels, and side moldings. Bertha was clean as a whistle. I started the engine, put "Whitney" in the deck, and rolled.

Our first destination was the Embarcadero for dinner, located on the waterfront a couple of miles away from Jack London Square. The lot was full as usual. I parked on the street and we walked in, arms connected at the elbows.

The maitre d' was a woman who appeared to be in her late forties. She had blond hair recently dyed and wore too much makeup. She had a pretty nice frame, but you knew she had mileage and would not age gracefully. Lines were already visible around her eyes, and since she probably showed off those big melons all her life, she'd be the last to know that wrinkled cleavage was certainly no turn-on.

We waited about fifteen minutes before our table was ready. After being seated, Cassandra commented, "This place is nice — I've never been here before."

The view of the waterfront was splendid. Houseboats of various sizes and shapes lit up the night, with people moving about oblivious to us diners. The water was rippling, with wave upon wave rushing up to the rocks right below us, only to roll back out peacefully. The bar area was full of yuppie types who would sit there, get drunk, lie to each other, then go home to some faithful housewife, claiming not to be hungry because of a business dinner while steadily pouring another drink. Looking around the restaurant, all I saw were smiling white faces. There was one other black couple seated on the opposite end of the room. I caught the brother's eye and gave him the "whatupGee" nod that only one black man to another really comprehends.

The few other blacks in the place were in groups of four or five co-workers (all white, one black) getting together after work to eat the free hors d'oeuvres and complain about the boss while nursing a single drink. These were the noisemakers who gave the eatery life. If you wanted a quiet, romantic dinner, you had to come later. Our waitress arrived with the menus, introduced herself, then said she would return in a few minutes.

Cassandra ordered steak and lobster, I chose prime rib. Our waitress, Debbie, asked if we wanted anything to drink while we waited for the main course. Cassandra ordered iced tea, and I replied that water would be cool. Debbie brought our drinks along with a loaf of bread, tray of butter, knife, cutting board, and two saucers.

I sliced bread as Cassandra lathered each piece with butter.

"So tell me about yourself," she prompted.

"My name is Reggie Alexander Jordan but everybody calls me 'Rainbow.' Twenty-seven years old, three brothers, one sister, grew up in the Saint John housing projects in Richmond, moved to Oaktown at thirteen, graduated with honors, lucked out and got a job with the City, been working there ever since."

"Come on, there's got to be more."

"Let's see, I'm a songwriter, like to read good books, enjoy tennis and ping pong — basically I'm a jack of all trades and master of none." I took a sip of water.

"What about the more personal stuff?" she asked, tilting her head slightly.

"I'm divorced."

"Children?"

"A six-year-old son whom I have custody of every other weekend, along with each summer."

"Is everything alright?" Debbie interrupted.

"Just fine," I responded.

"Your dinner will be served shortly."

"Thank you," we said in unison.

"You guys are a nice-looking couple," Debbie said as she sauntered away.

Once Debbie was out of earshot I resumed my rap, only this time the conversation was about her.

"I wish she would just bring our food and stop all the interruptions. See, she's doing this to guarantee herself a big tip." Cassandra smiled so I continued: "Look at her, bouncing around with her chest poked out, not realizing her nose is too big, legs too little, ass flatter than this cutting board, and hairs too straight. The girl looks like a fool."

Cassandra nearly choked on her bread laughing, but before I could continue my verbal assault, Debbie brought our salads.

"Deb, has anyone ever told you that you have the most beautiful eyes?" I asked with perfect seriousness.

"Yes," she smiled. "They say I have mom's eyes and daddy's features." She disappeared again.

"Now I know."

"You know what?" Cassandra asked.

"That her daddy has placed a very cruel curse on her ugly ass," I said, straight-faced.

"You're too much!" Cassandra laughed.

"What?" I asked, trying to look as innocent as possible.

Throughout dinner, each time Debbie passed our table Cassandra had to stifle her giggles. Naturally it would be after I made a wisecrack first. We finished only half our meal before realizing that we were stuffed, and wouldn't you know it, like toast, up popped Debbie.

"Will you two be needing a doggie bag?"

"That's fine," Cassandra responded.

"Okay, I'll be right back."

She bounced towards the kitchen to retrieve carry-out containers while I continued my comedy act on my date.

"It comes with the breeding. If it were me, I'd ask, 'Would you like a container for your leftovers?' However, if I looked like her, I'd probably say 'doggie bag' too."

Cassandra laughed so hard she almost fell out of her chair. Debbie returned with trays in hand, looked curiously at both of us, then burst out laughing with us, never knowing she was the butt of this joke.

"You guys are a happy couple, and you, sir, are a very funny guy," she stated.

"Oh," I arched my brow, "now comes the time when you give out false praise for a better tip, huh?"

"No, I really mean it."

"Thanks, Deb."

The bill for our dinner and drinks totaled sixty-seven dollars, so I gave Debbie a c-note and in my most eloquent of tones said, "Keep the change."

"Let's go," Cassandra giggled.

Grabbing me by the arm, she whisked me out of the restaurant. Once outside, she laughingly stated, "You, Mr. Jordan, are a fool."

"Call me Rainbow, baby — my mama do."

"Okay, Mr. Rainbow."

"And don't get used to this treatment."

"What treatment?"

"This big-money act I'm perpetrating. See, since I've attempted to play big shot with you, I'll be forced to eat at Mickey D's the rest of the week. The things a man got to do to fool a woman into believing he got money. . . ." I shrugged my shoulders.

"You're hilarious," Cassandra said as she pecked my cheek.

After opening the car door for her, I closed it, ran around to my side, got in, and rolled to our next destination. Since the weather was still a nice seventy-nine degrees, I opened the sunroof.

Executing a U-turn, I merged with traffic on 880 at 16th Street. As usual, big rigs hogged the road, spilling gravel and debris that bounced off the pavement. The ricochet effect resulted in numerous cracked windshields. If you attempted to pass, the air blasts they gave off would nearly blow you into the next lane.

Highway 880 — or the Nimitz Freeway, which is its official name — is known as the "danger zone" due to the fact that lives are lost daily. Cursing under my breath, I exited at 66th and informed Cassandra that we would be taking city streets the rest of the way. She could hardly care because she had no idea where we were going anyway.

As I zoomed past the Coliseum, we noticed the parking lot half full. That meant the Athletics baseball team had a game. As I hooked a right onto San Leandro Boulevard, Cassandra began talking.

"Do you ever go to the games?"

"Not really."

"Why not?" she pressed.

"I don't believe in wasting good money."

"Good money?"

"Honey, I cannot afford the ticket, parking fee, eats, or drinks. I mean, four dollars for a watered-down sixteen-ounce glass of beer is ridiculous. See, the owners — most of whom never played a lick of sports in their life — pay athletes millions of dollars for bragging rights to say their team is the best. Then, in order to make money, the team owners jack the price onto the consumer, us, the fans."

"You sound jealous of athletes."

"Not at all, they should make every dime they can because once they hit mid-thirties, the elite at that, the owners will kick them to the curb. Understand this, TV makes people think sports is important, when in actuality, it's just a game. Now three blocks from here you can find homeless dope fiends, kids who can't read .... Nobody gives a damn about that 'cause some sorry-ass owner wants to say my team is best. Plus, now there is no loyalty."

"What do you mean?"

"What I mean is, when I was a boy, your superstar played for your team until his career was damn near over. Today, with free agency, one guy will play for a different team six straight years — there's no consistency. It's like every year you root for a different team without having loyalty to any of them. The players go where the money's at and I don't blame them, it's the nature of the beast."

"I'll take you to a music concert then," Cassandra said, sighing.

I grinned while continuing on to the next stop of our journey.

2
THE PLan

"Yo, pass da wine, foo!"

"Awight Buckey, jus lemme git one mo' sip."

As Spodie lifted the bottle of wine to his mouth, Buckey hurled an ashtray directly at his chest. The deadly thud brought everyone to immediate attention and served as a reminder just who was in charge.

Buckey Jones was a fool in every sense of the word. Even his closest friends on occasion could not escape his fury. His given name was Curtis, but only family and a few select friends would dare call him that.

Standing a mere five feet nine inches, one hundred and eighty pounds, with a powerful build from years of incarceration. Buckey was not the tallest nor best built in the hood but had a rep and temper granting him project legend status.

He had a three-inch afro always done in cornrows,

mustache covering big lips, and a goatee. Not really ugly, but you wouldn't want him going out with your daughter, either. A known fact throughout the hood was if you wanted something sinister done to someone, Buckey was the man.

Lately Buckey had been turning down "jobs" due to a burning desire to be a drug lord.

The house where Buckey's gang usually met was a dilapidated two-story Victorian on 10th & Chestnut, rented to his woman Violet Harris. Five eleven held up by a skinny one hundred-and-twenty-pound frame, Violet was rail-thin. She had a nice butt and big breasts, but her face and legs displayed scratches, scars, and discolorations on them from the frequent beatings administered by her man.

Her teeth were rotten, with one in front chipped and black holes throughout where cavities needed fixing. Once-upon-a-time nice hair was now a gold-dyed mess with black new growth shamelessly visible.

Violet worshipped the ground Buckey walked on, and to him she was a movie star. They made a very odd couple, fighting and arguing all the time, jealous of each other when in actuality nobody else wanted either of them. However, when push came to shove, Violet and Buckey were the ghetto version of Bonnie and Clyde.

Their house was a bonafide shack with front steps rotted, railings loose and in desperate need of repair, windowpanes on the door cracked, and the entire place reeking of urine. Violet could care less about homemaking, and it showed.

Dirty clothes, days-old food, empty liquor bottles, beer cans, and cigarette butts were strewn throughout. The sofa and loveseat were of the four-pieces-for-a-hundred-and-ninety-nine-dollar variety, coffee table a scarred-up disaster, and with no cable, the TV produced a coarse-grain picture.

The dining room table was a hand-me-down left by the previous tenants, chairs torn and ragged. The kitchen sink stayed full of dirty dishes, and roaches paraded around as if they owned the place.

Tenants such as Violet had the neighborhood home-owners' association regretting the day that the Acorn, Campbell Village, and Mo'House projects were built. That development forced decent working-class people to move away from a once-proud area of the city that had decayed to the point where absentee landlords were the order of the day.

Pouring beer into an ashtray occupied by a roach and laughing while it drowned, Buckey nodded his head to Too $horts' latest single, "Freaky Tales." With his sorry crew present, he laid out his master plan. When he spoke, all his flunkeys listened.

"Slack, blow his ass away soon as you see da whites of his eyes."

Slack was the triggerman. They used to call him "High-pockets" because when he walked the two back pockets on his trousers touched each other. However, Buckey nicknamed him Slack, short for Slackass.

Cream-colored, skinny, and innocent-looking, Slack didn't strike fear into anyone by his appearance. But no

one messed with him either, because Slack would shoot
you in a minute. He dealt in stolen guns, so his criminal
activities were never traced.

There were numerous murders that five-o, the Oaktown Police, attributed to Slack but couldn't pin on him
because he didn't talk. Diarrhea of the mouth was something he didn't have. His vices were booze and weed —
nothing else mattered.

> *I met this girl, her name was Karen*
> *she kept lookin, while I kept starin*
> *baby came thru wit mah homeboy Derin*
> *her booty was stuffed in da jeans she was wearin*
> *she never left, he cut out*
> *I know you all know what I'm talkin about*

"Earl, you break 'im. Take da jewelry, scrill, an dose
Air Jordans dat fool be wearin."

Earl Robinson was a thief. Homes, cars, department
stores, it didn't matter. If it had value, Earl would steal
it. High yellow with jet-black curly hair, he was slim and
sneaky. There could be a group of homeys shooting the
breeze when all of a sudden you'd realize that Earl was
standing next to you, grinning.

You wouldn't know how long he'd been there or how he
managed to get right up on you undetected, but that was
his trademark. He liked Old English beer and fat women,
the bigger the better. Everyone would laugh at some of
the broads Earl showed up with, but he didn't care.

He'd just casually state, "I ain't got ta be jealous 'cause

she so big don't nobody want her BUT me, and since it's like that, she treats me like a king." Then he would produce that familiar grin while fading into the crowd. Before you realized it, Earl would be gone.

"Spodie, make sho yo sorry-ass lemon ain't da reason we get busted."

Still rubbing his chest from the pain of Buckey's ashtray, Spodie just lowered his head. He was the coward of the bunch, but also one of the best mechanics in the projects. Gifted with the ability to make a decent living fixing cars, he threw it away due to a burning desire to hang out and be accepted by common thugs like Buckey. Spodie was a misfit among this band of lunatics, but since he always had some beat-up jalopy to ride in, they welcomed him with open arms.

James "Spodie" McKnight was not a small man, standing six foot three and weighing two hundred and sixty pounds. When not working on cars, his daily routine consisted of watching TV, drinking beer, and eating. This lack of activity resulted in a pot belly, soft arms, and very little stamina. Twenty-eight years old, he still lived with his mama. To all who knew him, he was a big baby.

"Violet, when Earl gib you da money, you make sho it get ta me."

Violet nodded the affirmative so Buckey continued.

"Dis shit gone put us on da map, let all dem fools know we ain't ta be fuccked wit, y'all wit me?"

It was a sorry pep speech, but for Buckey's gang of fools it worked. They all agreed with his plan.

3
THE DATE

Bogie's parking lot was full, and so was the adjacent bank lot, for that matter. Getting lucky and parking across the street from the club, I got out, stepped to the other side, and opened the door. With fingers interlocked, Cassandra and I walked up to the entrance.

The outside resembled a country-western bar with shellacked wood and a giant neon sign proudly displaying the club name. We entered, only to be greeted by two large football types who motioned for us to "spread 'em." Extending our arms, we were scanned with metal detectors.

Next, we had to produce legitimate identification. No ID, no get in. Cassandra's party purse was searched before we were allowed entrance. She found this sequence of events amusing.

"See, that keeps out the riff-raff," she said.

There was no fee for Cassandra since ladies were admitted free, so I paid the seven-dollar cover and we both went inside the club area. Once in, the first thing that caught your attention was the bar, which ran the entire length of the place. It had fifteen evenly placed stools with a mirror spanning the distance so you could sit there and see everything going on behind you.

To the immediate right sat two video games with the restrooms nearby. Next to the restrooms was an area that always said "reserved" but never was. It had six square tables with four chairs each, along with the entire wall lined by a padded bench.

Directly in front of the reserved seating area was the stage and dance floor. There was space for forty people to dance comfortably but it always seemed like sixty were out there. The minute you began to get a groove, some fool would trounce on your shoes or bump you out of step.

It was not uncommon to see people dancing right in front of their table on the carpet. To the right of the dance floor and stage was the main seating area, with twelve tables and forty-eight chairs.

Wednesday nights were on hits, not only because it was oldie-but-goodie night, but also due to the singing contest, with a band that could accompany you and play any song you wanted to croon.

Contestants would bring a cassette tape of the song they wanted to sing, and after the band rehearsed it a few times, the prospective singer would be called into a back room to practice. If the wannabe couldn't blow, "Slade" would tell them to come back next week.

Slade was the leader of the band and at forty-five the

eldest. Milky Way black with a receding hairline, he stood a meager five feet five inches and possessed uncanny ability on drums.

Having played backup for numerous superstars, Slade considered this gig just another job. However, as a professional he did take it seriously. The band's entire repertoire consisted of rhythm and blues, top 40, and disco music. Slade sang most of the songs and did so with precision.

Escorting Cassandra to the reserved seating area, I mumbled something about having to pay my water bill then walked away. Stopping to greet many of the happy faces I knew, I spotted Slade and handed him my tape.

"Slade, I want on the show. I got people here from Capitol Records, man — if they like me, they sign me," I lied.

"Rainbow, that's a bet, but you need to know that all the heavyweights are on the show tonight hoping for the same dream as you."

"I ain't worried about that, just put me on."

"Cool," he said, accepting my tape then heading for the back room.

Returning to our table, I took Cassandra's hand and led her to the dance floor. The DJ was playing the slow Heatwave tune "Always and Forever." Pulling close, we began a sensuous bump 'n grind. She held on very tightly while telling me how much she enjoyed this date.

Looking directly into her eyes, I gave her a loving kiss as my hands wandered greedily over her assets. It was then that I knew we'd do the knotty tonight. ConFunkShun's "Fun, Fun, Fun" blared over the sound system, which caused everyone to display their best dance moves. Eyeing each other to see if our skills were tight, which they were, we returned to our seat winded and sweaty.

Normally the singing contest started around midnight, but since it was rare to have so many talented people perform on the same night, the show started at eleven.

It was known that all the top-line singers would first see who was on the show before committing. The fifty-dollar first prize, twenty-five second, or fifteen third wasn't the issue. Bragging rights counted more than any monetary figure, so generally the most talented did not perform against one another. Tonight would prove to be different because at stake was a possible recording contract. Slade grabbed the mike and began his spiel.

"Y'all ready to see the best of the bay?"

"Yeah!" the crowd roared.

"Entertained royally?"

"Yeah!"

"Are you ready for the talent competition to begin?"

"Yeah!"

"Ladies and gentlemen, only the most talented are allowed to compete, so sit back, relax, and enjoy as Bogie's presents to you our weekly talent search. First up is my man Savvy."

Slade took his position on drums as Savvy walked onstage. With a trim muscular build, Louisville cut, and two-piece green Italian suit, Savvy was smashing. One thick rope draped his neck and two large rings were proudly displayed on his fingers as he gripped the microphone.

He wore no shirt, which accented his awesome frame.

As he gave shouts to his folks, the band began playing. The tune was Tony Toni Tone's "Whatever You Want." Savvy, with his silky-smooth voice, blew it away. The crowd went ballistic.

"Baby, he's good! I need to tell my sister about this place," Cassandra screamed above the din.

Next up was Harvey, who was decked out in blue slacks, matching blue shoes, and a white torso-clinging sweater that complemented his powerful physique.

A former pro roller skater, his legs were as thick as his arms. Harvey began singing Earth, Wind, & Fire's love tune "Reasons," hitting all those Phillip Bailey falsettos. The women were beside themselves, screaming at the top of their lungs, while I sat there thinking what a fool I'd make of myself tonight. I knew I was not on the level of these guys.

After Harvey finished, Paradise strutted out. She resided in Vallejo but had many relatives and friends in Oaktown. The girl was short, had a beautiful behind, trim waist, baseball-sized tits, and wore a form-fitting purple dress. She looked radiant. As she blew "Sweet Thang" it seemed like the roof would blast off the joint.

Paradise was so good the men in the audience began showering the stage with balled-up fives, tens, and twenties. By the time she finished, she'd picked up at least a hundred and fifty dollars.

Savvy and Harv weren't tripping because they knew the brothers were doing that only to spite them. It was the jealousy factor: the dudes didn't like the fact that their women enjoyed the men's voices, so they tried to help the females win.

After the folks in the audience caught their breath, Lionel appeared onstage. The house "ringer," Lionel should have been famous years ago but somehow it just hadn't materialized. The band usually made it a practice to never sing background for anyone, but tonight they did so for all the contestants.

Lionel started with a spiel of "Yeah, let's give all the performers a hand. I'd like ta say it's hard gettin up here doin this, but we're givin it our all. Y'all ready ta rock?"

With that said, he blew Marvin Gaye's "Let's Get It On." And blow he did. The boy was professional in every sense of the word. You knew if he didn't win, something was wrong, because for a five-minute song Lionel took twenty.

Every nuance was accentuated by the band hitting a "bamp," meaning he obviously had practiced with them on more than one occasion. However, all in all, the brother could blow, there was no denying that.

Once Lionel finished, KeKe walked out. KeKe Ah Tay was his stage name, and the dude took a back seat to no one. It seemed like KeKe was always running the lake, but he still stayed slightly overweight. Midnight-black with a round face, he was dressed in black slacks, white turtleneck sweater, and two-toned black and white alligator boots.

Giving the band its cue, KeKe sang Teddy Pendergrass's "Turn Off the Lights." The boy had range, stage presence, and a booming voice. Everyone knew he was Lionel's equal if not more, so by now the crowd was thoroughly entertained. Much to their delight, the show still wasn't over.

People milled about the crowd debating whether Lionel or KeKe should win as "Pru" walked out and lifted the mic from its stand. Built like a brick shithouse, Pru was stunning. She wore a turquoise leather mini skirt proudly showing off tree-trunk thighs. With a matching waist-length jacket zipped only halfway to the top, her large breasts seemed as though they would pop out at any moment.

The women became silent as the men hooted and yelled. Pru sang "Neither One of Us" by Gladys Knight through a deep husky voice that was perfect for the tune. Although most of the brothers were too busy checking out her legs, ass, and titties to care whether she had talent or not, she sang the hell out of that song. As she neared the end, I told Cassandra, "Baby, I'll be right back."

When Pru exited the stage, I walked out, snatching the mic like I owned it. My entrance caught Cassandra totally off guard, because while staring at her I began my spiel.

"I'd like to thank Bogie's for giving me the opportunity to display my talent. You see, music is from the soul and once it dies, a part of us dies with it."

> *I've been watching you, for so very long,*
> *trying ta get my nerve built up ta be so strong.*
> *I really want ta meet you, but I'm kinda scared,*
> *cause you're the kind of lady, with so much class. . . .*

I get my thoughts together, for the very next day
but when I see you lady, I forget what ta say.
Your eyes and hair, such a beautiful tone,
the way you dress and walk, it really turns me
  oonnnn, yeah,
Ooh you really turn me on, come on — come on —
come on.

I hooked up Jodeci's "Come and Talk to Me" straight from the heart. While maybe a notch below the rest of the performers, tonight I was equal. Singing a very popular new hit while everyone else went old school gave me an edge.

The entire time I sang, my attention was focused on my date, whose face could have lit up the room. Remaining onstage, I was joined by the other performers. Slade took the mic and stated, "If I touch you, that means you should go find your seat."

With that he proceeded to touch me, Savvy, and Pru. I didn't care because my game was to impress Cassandra and it worked like a charm. When I returned to our table she gave me a loving hug along with a very sensuous kiss, letting everyone know that she was with me. Pru and Savvy exited the platform steaming.

Judging of the four remaining contestants was so tight they had to have a sing-off. This meant each person would sing parts of another song. Grabbing her by the hand, I told Cassandra, "Let's go."

"Wait," she said, "I wanna see who wins."

"It's midnight, Cinderella, you got a job tomorrow, so let's bounce."

She reluctantly followed my lead as we made our way to the exit. Before we got there Paradise started singing Natalie Cole's romantic cut "Inseparable."

As we walked slowly through the parking lot with our fingers entwined, Cassandra blurted out, "It seemed like you were singing just for me. I didn't know you could blow like that."

After I unlocked her door, I pulled her into my arms, sticking my tongue deep inside her throat. The kiss was wonderful and lasted the better part of a full minute. Helping her into the car, I jogged around to my side and we rolled.

4
THE Hit

The corner of 14th and Peralta was at its chaotic best, with a gang of fools hanging as usual. Drug transactions took place everywhere, along with drinking and getting high.

On one corner sat a laundromat packed with women washing clothes while their dirty children ran in and out playing tag. Next to that was a liquor store with so many fools hanging out that if you weren't from the area or ghetto-raised, you'd pass it up in search of another.

To the right an Oriental greasy spoon served up whopping doses of fried rice, chow mein, burgers, fries, and cheesesteak sandwiches. Across the street was another corner store that made the majority of its scrill selling booze.

Directly across from this store was "King Narciss's"

church. He was famous for the slogan "It's Nice To Be Nice," and since the temple always provided the less fortunate with free food and clothing, that corner remained clean as a whistle twenty-four seven. Even the poorest of blacks respect religion.

The remainder of the block stayed dirty, with vagrants getting high, drinking, or sitting in beat-up hooptie talking about fame and fortune. You could buy heroin, cocaine, dank, pills, food stamps, or stolen merchandise, paying fifty cents on the dollar or less. Some of the prices were so low they may as well have given it to you.

Young thuggish types would be handsomely paid as lookouts, and upon spotting the police would yell out FIVE-O or ROLLER ON THE SET! When that happened, everyone on the corner scattered like roaches when an unexpected light is flicked on in the middle of the night.

Stoney waltzed into the diner, ordering dry-fried ribs along with a soda to wash it down. Copping a squat, he ate his grub while surveying the set outside until the coast was clear and the man gone.

The biggest fish on the corner, it was nothing for him to pay off some idiot with rocks or cash to commit felonious acts against rival dealers or folks who forgot to pay off a credit tab. Stoney wanted all the money, and if you peddled on his turf, you bought product from him, period.

Stoney had a thing for athletic apparel. Today he wore a black nylon sweatsuit with Air Jordans, matching t-shirt displaying the swoosh logo, Raider jacket and cap, along with several humongous pieces of jewelry. Every day he wore a different-colored sweatsuit and always had on matching accessories, from sneakers to golf cap. Many people wondered why he usually wore big coats even when it was eighty degrees outside.

Blessed with the gift for gab, Stoney was a smooth talker, a real ladies' man. He always garnered the best the projects had to offer because the guy reeked of money. Spotting two fine tenders wearing mini skirts and high heels, he put his mack game to work.

"Hey Doris, let me have a minute uh yo time."

Doris pirouetted on her heels like a stallion on display at an equine auction. Nineteen years young and blessed with a beautiful bosom, long legs, and a nubian face, she was proud that Stoney would choose her.

"Baby," he said, "you make me weaker than Superman playing with kryptonite. Check dis out, why don't you come back here in 'bout an hour an kick it wit me?"

Normally Stoney watched his corner like a hawk, only dropping his game while rapping to a honey. That's why he failed to notice an old gray-primed Chevy pull up on the block and two of its occupants get out, heading in his direction.

"I know what you aftah," Doris shouted, "so why didn't you invite Yvette too?"

"Look, baby, I ain't interested in Yvette."

He heard a scream and saw people scatter, but it was too late. Slack put the Uzi up to his temple and fired. Stoney's blood splattered against the store window as he went down in a heap.

He was dead before his head bounced on the dirty pavement. To cause pandemonium, Slack began firing in the air, at cars rolling by, store windows — he was shooting just for the hell of it.

People ran in all directions ducking for cover. Doris stood paralyzed in a state of shock, shaking down to her spine. Since she was frozen in her tracks, Yvette grabbed her by the arm and jerked her inside the liquor store.

Throughout the chaos, Earl crouched low and worked Stoney over. He took rings off fingers, ropes from the neck, base rocks and wads of cash from coat pockets. To the casual observer it appeared that Earl was grieving the death of a friend.

To the trained eye, Earl stole everything Stoney possessed. Jerking the sneakers off the dead man's feet, Earl shouted to Slack "Let's raise!" with both men then sprinting to the corner and hopping in as Spodie pulled away from the curb.

Once the police, paramedics, and fire trucks arrived, people began coming back out from their hiding spots. With beat officers trying unsuccessfully to get people to talk, a solitary figure watched the entire process from the shadows of the church. He appeared to be waiting for the bus, but as they came and went he remained stationary.

Sergeant Nathan Johnson was the lead detective. A very large black man, he stood six foot six, weighed three hundred pounds, and took his job seriously. Working his way up through the ranks, Johnson rightfully earned every promotion. Due to the fact of being black, he had to be twice as good as white cops just to get the same recognition.

His partner was a Chicano named Manny Hernandez. Mexicans throughout the city labeled Hernandez a sell-out because, coming from the barrios, they assumed he would represent them well.

The Latino community hosted block parties, dedications, and numerous ceremonies commending Hernandez for being an asset to their race. Once he married and started talking and acting white, the community was outraged.

It was known that Hernandez, short and stocky with a bad attitude, would rough you up in a minute whenever he knew he could get away with it.

Johnson began questioning Yvette while Doris received treatment for shock, all the while staring at Stoney's covered-up body and crying loudly.

"Okay, let's start from the beginning. What did you see?"

"We didn't see shit," stated Yvette defiantly.

"Look, young lady, you had to see something because it all went down right in front of you."

Johnson was immediately irritated with Yvette's flippity mouth but knew that no one would talk tonight for fear of being tagged a snitch. Getting Doris and Yvette's phone numbers and addresses, he promised the girls that they would be hearing from him real soon. That done, he and his partner headed back to the station.

Buckey strode across the street from the church and casually asked, "What happened?"

By now word on the street had it that the mob called the hit on Stoney because he got too big for his britches. People who weren't even there gave vivid descriptions of the killing, along with fabricated embellishments and their own version of why it happened.

Buckey smiled broadly, knowing that no one would talk for fear of retaliation, and that the more preposterous the stories became, the colder five-o's trail would get. Satisfied, he strolled down the street to his hooptie and went to the crib. Barging in the front door still grinning, he said to his assembled gang, "Good job, y'all — dat fool never knew what hit 'im."

Everyone smiled, satisfied that their leader was pleased.

"Now what we gotta do is lay low so's we don't cause 'spicion. Spodie, you da weak lank, so keep yo ass incognito til ah say it be cool, dig?"

"I hear ya, Buck," Spodie answered.

Buckey wasn't worried about Slack, Earl, or Violet but knew if five-o applied pressure, Spodie would crack. He made a mental note to keep an eye on that clown.

The take amounted to nine thousand in cash, four in dope, a zip-lock bag full of jewelry, and the sneakers.

"Earl, yo ass is cool, ah could'na done it bettah mahself, shidd...."

Earl smiled sheepishly, proud to be at the peak of his game, and Buckey noticed. Buckey handed each member fifteen hundred dollars while pocketing three grand. Spodie, realizing the figures didn't quite add up, blurted out, "Hey Buckey, nine thousand divided by five is eighteen hundred apiece."

Like a lightning bolt Buckey slapped him so hard on the face that his hand print was visible for all to see.

"Fool, if anybody should be complainin it should be Earl or Slack — dey did all da work while you ain't did shit but drove. Yo ass should be lucky you gettin dat. Get da fuck outta heah."

Spodie scooped up his money and ran to the door, not bothering to close it. Laughing loudly while locking the door, Buckey told his crew, "Help me bag dis shit up."

Breaking off sections of base rock, he passed out portions to the other three and they went to work. When he looked up, Earl was gone.

"Fit ta give dat shit ta some fat-ass hoe," he laughed while admiring Earl's Houdini act.

"Buck, ah'll see you tomorrow." Slack rose to leave.

"Awight Slackaroni, don't spin it all in one place."

With that said, Slack was gone. Violet was busily chopping and bagging rocks for sale when an idea struck her man.

"Come on, baby, dare's one mo thang ah gotta do, let's go."

Violet grabbed her coat, following obediently as Buckey marched out.

PLeasure and Pain

The drive home from Bogie's was pleasant, with Cassandra yakking all the way. She kept repeating how much fun she had and what a great show she'd seen. All I did was smile, basking in the limelight along with feeling pretty good about the praise she lavished upon me. Pulling up in front of her building, I turned off the ignition.

"Baby, I had a cool time with you and really hope we can do it again soon."

"Rainbow, I'd love to spend more time with you."

"Check this out, I'm not seeing anyone right now but would like to see a lot of you."

"I feel the same way," she said.

"Fine as you are, it's hard for me to believe you don't have a significant other."

"It's by choice. Come on, walk me to my door."

I got out and walked around to her side, but she was already out of the car. Nabbing her leftover food from the back seat, I closed the door and activated the alarm. We walked slowly to her door with our arms around each other's waist.

"Do you have time to come in?"

"Yes," I answered.

"Good. I don't want to give my nosy neighbor anything to talk about."

We entered her unit and placed the "doggie bag" on the kitchen table. Turning on her heels she approached while staring wickedly into my eyes.

"You, Mr. Jordan, are a very handsome man."

Before I could reply she covered my mouth with hers, kissing me passionately. My manhood rose to full attention immediately. The more heat we generated, the bolder my hands became, working her dress until it sat halfway up her behind.

Locating the wetness I desired, I stroked her moist cunt with deliberate precision. A soft moan escaped her lips, which gave me the incentive needed to pull her panties to the side and insert my finger into her box.

Pulling my lips away from hers, I kissed her cheeks, neck, shoulders, then made my way to her breasts. With her nipples now at full attention too, I laid her down on the sofa, placing my beef directly over her soaking split.

Kissing her greedily, my fingers worked over her love canal, not giving her time to breathe. As Cassandra wiggled and squirmed, my tongue worked its magic on her navel and inner thighs. Gently tugging off her undies, I plunged my tongue into her prized possession, which caused her to gasp wildly for air.

I hungrily licked, lapped, and munched on her clit until she let out a loud scream. Her river flowed freely and she lay perfectly still, looking at me through glassy eyes.

"Take me," she said throatily.

Leaving a trail of clothing behind, we went into her bedroom. She sprawled out on the bed with legs wide open in anticipation. I pulled off my briefs and watched with delight as her eyes grew large as saucers.

"That looks very good. I don't know if I can handle it."

Without saying a word, I positioned myself over her and penetrated. Using slow deliberate strokes, I pulled almost out only to drive back in deeper. Working in circular motions, I stirred it up like coffee. She began singing the love song I enjoy hearing.

"Oh . . . Ah . . . Umm . . . Unh . . . Ooh . . . Baby . . . yes . . . Oh yes . . . Oh. Ahhhh . . . ."

Placing my inner thighs on the outside of her legs, I rose on toes and elbows then proceeded to submarine in and out until she came violently. As she lost control, she let out a guttural moan that appeared to come from another room.

It was the same sound Eddie Murphy makes jokes about, the kind where the woman falls in love immediately. Returning to the missionary position, I gave her all my power. I was trying to push my meat through her heart, and she was loving every bit of it. Sweat poured off our bodies like a running faucet.

Cassandra began kissing my chest, shoulders, arms, any place her lips could find. My juice, which had been bubbling for a while, finally exploded. The eruption was so powerful that she held on for dear life.

We lay entwined in each other's arms for a very long time, connected like Siamese twins. After catching my breath, I eventually went to take a shower.

The bathroom was tastefully decorated in black, just like the rest of the house. I dried off, put on my clothes, and returned to the bedroom to say goodnight. Cassandra was out like a light, looking content.

Lifting one rose from the vase, I placed it on her pillow. Next I reentered the kitchen and put her leftovers into the refrigerator before walking out the door.

The cool air was refreshing, prompting me to stretch my tired body. Heading towards Bertha, I spotted a beat-up Sedan de Ville parked behind me with an ugly broad behind the wheel. Silently wondering what she was up to, I peeped a dude heading in her direction.

"Hey homes," he greeted me.

"Whatup, Gee."

As I walked by he stole on me. The force of the blow knocked me down.

"What the fuck you . . . ."

His foot to my face stopped my words in mid-sentence, causing me to bite my tongue. Falling backwards, I covered up as blows rained on my head. They were coming in a blur, at least seven or eight, too many to count.

Out of the corner of my eye I saw him raise his foot, preparing to stomp me. Using all the force I could muster,

I hit him with an uppercut to the nuts. Once he doubled over, I rose to my feet, now ready to rumble.

Connecting with another uppercut that would have made Holyfield proud, I caught him on the chin, dropping him like a hot potato. He scrambled to his feet and ran to the car. His lady pulled off but suddenly stopped in front of me.

I dodged the beer bottle he hurled at me, ducking as it broke on the concrete. In an icy voice he stated, "Keep yo ass way from Sandra, muthafucka."

"Get yo ass out the car and finish the job, fool, come on!"

They burned rubber, pulling off with tires squealing. Porch lights flickered on as residents peered through curtains. I got in Bertha and drove off toward home. My mind raced wildly with many questions.

Who was that? What did he do that shit for? How did he know I was with Cassandra? Why didn't my usual alert senses warn me of possible danger? What kind of people did she keep company with? I would get my answers, but right now I just wanted to go home. Pulling onto my block, I became aware that my body was stiff and my face sore from all the happenings of the night.

I live on Agua Vista Street, which is one block long, located in the heart of East Oaktown. My block is surrounded by High Street, 38th, Lyons, and Santa Rita. It's a nice, quiet, tree-lined street full of homes built to last, unlike many of the newer tract homes sprouting up around the country.

I own a cool single-level two-bedroom which, although

not fancily decorated, is mine. After easing up the driveway, I got out and headed for the back gate. As I opened it
Iceberg bum-rushed me.

Named after the player Iceberg Slim, my dog is a pure-
bred German shepherd with jet-black hair and gold-col-
ored splotches around the eyes and ears. I'd spent good
money having him trained at K9 school, so not only was
he an excellent guard dog, he was also house-trained.

"Missed me, didn't you, boy?"

"Woof!"

"Let's get you something to drink."

After filling his pan with water from the hose, I went
inside my crib. Iceberg shadowed me in, and sensing something wrong, he started whining.

"It's alright, Berg, I'm cool."

Iceberg stood there with tail wagging and head down,
sniffing me. Getting a glass out of the cupboard, I filled
it with warm water then added salt. Stirring it up I headed
for the bathroom, where I gurgled and washed my mouth
out.

My tongue burned severely from the salt. Turning, I
filled the tub with water and soap then did what I had
avoided all the way home. I looked in the mirror to survey
the damage. My face resembled a purple onion, with dried-
up blood caked on my lip. Taking off my clothes, I noticed
that my pants had a hole in the knee. Now *that* pissed
me off.

"Motherfucker!" I yelled, "Yo ass gone pay for this!"

It was hard enough for me to stack a wardrobe, let
alone have some fool assist me with ruining it. He would

definitely pay for this shit. Hopping in the tub, I washed off the blood, scrubbed the dirt, got out, then toweled off.

After taking two aspirin for my splitting headache, I pulled back the covers and got in bed, dozing off as soon as my head hit the pillow. My sleep didn't last long, because after what seemed like only minutes, my phone rang off the hook. The clock displayed 7 AM.

"Hello."

"Rainbow, it's me, Mommy."

"Hey Mom, what's up?"

"Yo brutha's done got hisself kilt."

"Who?" I sat up.

"Ricky, he was shot lass night, everybody's heah."

"Momma, I'm on my way."

A FOOL WiTH MONEY

"Kicked dat square's ass, huh?"

"Yeah baby, you was beatin him down," Violet responded.

"If ah would'na slipped, ah was bout ta stomp da livin shit out da muthafucka."

"It musta been somethin on da groun, babes."

"Yeah, ah know, ah slipped on it."

"You want me ta go home?" she asked.

"Hell naw, go ta Fo'teenth and Peralta."

"Ta what?"

"Look bitch, jus drive."

"Ah got yo bitch, bastahd."

"Yeah, an you gone give it ta me ta-nite."

Buckey roared at his own spontaneous wit while Violet drove to the spot. She could care less what he was up to as long as he kept his promise once they got home.

At such a late hour, 14th and Peralta was quiet like the calm before the storm. Violet eased the Caddy in front of the laundromat and parked. Buckey put on latex gloves, grabbed Stoney's kicks from under the seat, got out, then threw them up and over the telephone line. On the third try he hit his mark, with the tennis shoes dangling over the wires. In the ghetto this gesture is meant as respect for a fallen soldier, but to Buckey it was a symbol of dis-respect. Satisfied, he got back in the car.

"Run me by Spodie's block, ah wanna see what dat foo's up to."

"Okay baby."

Violet started up the engine. As she cruised off, Buckey opened a bottle of beer, drinking sloppily.

"Ya know da reason ah thowed dose shoes up dare was fa all dese wannabe foos ta know det dat same shit gone happen ta dem if dey ain't on dey p's an q's."

Violet hooked a left on Adeline Street.

"I'ont trust Spodie."

"Why not?"

"Spodie run his mouf too much. He subject ta do some-thin stupid wif his bank and lead five-o right to us. I'm gone hafta tail his ass fo da next few days."

Violet turned left on 32nd, went up two blocks, then made another left on Union, parking in front of Poplar Recreation Center. This area of the city was known as "Dogtown."

Spodie lived with his mother right across from the park. Their home was similar to most in the neighborhood, a shack. Beat-up cars and parts lined the driveway, along with spilled motor oil and trash strewn throughout.

Spending most of his days at the rec center playing ping pong, dominoes, cards, or shooting pool, Spodie was a big kid at heart. The center itself was small compared to most but possessed a dedicated staff, numerous programs, and great community support.

Surrounded entirely by an eight-foot chain-link fence, the center consisted of a sandbox with swings, basketball court on rough gravel, tiny baseball field, and several benches under shade trees. Behind the building was an additional sandbox play area with picnic tables.

The only activity going on in Spodie's house came from a flickering TV set in his mother's room. More than likely, the screen watched her. Out back in the garage there was a light on, which meant one thing — Spodie was up to something. Buckey finished his beer then tossed the bottle in the back. The inside of the car was just as filthy as their home.

"Lemme go see what dat foo's up to," he said.

Buckey got out. Moving swiftly, he went to the back of the garage and peered through a dirty window. What he saw nearly caused him to burst out laughing, which would have blown his game.

He momentarily turned away from the window to stifle his laugh, then returned. There, leaning up against a car receiving a blow job, was Spodie. Buckey recognized the girl as a hooker named Flossie who plied her trade on San Pablo Avenue.

Just as predicted, Spodie was squandering the money already. Laying her down on an old car seat in the corner, Spodie put on a condom and began screwing her. Buckey licked his lips grinning as Flossie faked moans.

43

She was telling Spodie how good it felt, all the while looking bored as hell. It was over as fast as it began, with Spodie's body stiffening up then him pulling out and removing the rubber.

Popping the tab on a can of beer and feeling real good about himself, Spodie started blabbering while Flossie hurried to get dressed. The sooner she got back to her corner, the quicker she could find another trick to turn.

Buckey's attention was on Flossie, who wore too much makeup but did have a nice frame. As he stared at her vagina, his hand snaked inside his pants, stroking his penis until it became rock hard. But the more Spodie talked, the quicker Buckey's dick went limp.

"Yeah baby, I'ma be a big man real soon," Spodie boasted.

"How's that?" Flossie asked, not really giving a damn.

"Me an mah boys gone take over the dope trade in West Oh."

"Really."

"That's right, we bumped off this fool tonight, hit his ass proper."

Buckey was enraged, gripping the windowsills tightly.

"Look, man, I got a job to do and time is money, so if you ain't spendin no moe, take me back where you found me, okay?"

"Walk yo ass back, bitch."

Flossie picked up a tire iron and flung it wildly in Spodie's direction then dashed out the door. Spodie laughed heartily before continuing to enjoy his brew.

Violet saw the prostitute running from the garage. Mistakenly thinking that Buckey was giving away what was rightfully hers, she got out and headed to the back steaming. Spodie lifted the can to his mouth then choked at what he saw. Buckey stood in the doorway looking pissed.

"Man, what da fuck you doin tellin dat bitch mah bizness."

"Buckey, I didn't tell her nothin."

"You a goddamn liar — ah heard yo ass wif mah own two ears."

Violet appeared, demanding, "Buckey, what da fuck goin on in here?"

"Baby, dis fool tellin dat skeezoid what we done did ta-nite."

"Naw Buckey, you got it wrong, man, I ain't said shit."

Buckey grabbed a baseball bat propped against the wall and rushed in towards Spodie.

"Buckey, wait!" Spodie pleaded while trying to get up.

Buckey swung wildly, hitting Spodie's arm, which he used to protect his face.

"Buck, wait man, I didn't do it!"

The second swing connected solidly with Spodie's dome, causing him to fall to the floor as blood gushed from his eye. Next, he felt a searing pain to his rib cage, which cracked on impact.

Spodie reached for the tire iron and swung backhanded, hitting Buckey on the legs and making him lose his balance. Violet stood still, biting what few fingernails she had remaining. Spodie swung again but missed.

Buckey bounced to his feet, swinging with fury. Hitting Spodie on the head and face at least ten times, he broke the bat in two from the deadly force used. Spodie's corpse oozed brain matter all over the garage floor.

Rifling through Spodie's pockets, Buckey took his remaining cash, fourteen hundred. Picking up the bat handle along with a couple of beers, he grabbed Violet by the arm and ran to the car.

Violet got in while Buckey went to the center's dumpster. Placing the bat handle inside a paper bag, he stuffed it in the bin.

He knew the trash would be emptied at six that morning, eliminating any incriminating evidence against him. The dumpster had a padlock on it but he still managed to lift the corner just enough for the bag to fit.

"Take me home, girl — ta-maura I'ma let all dem foos know ah got dope fa sale."

Violet drove home horny as hell. She knew when Buckey did crazy shit like this, his sexual appetite would be starving, and tonight, she would damn sure feed her man.

Running through flashing yellow lights on Adeline without slowing down, she veered left on 10th and eased into their driveway.

"Now you can take care of that itch you was talkin bout," she laughed.

"Ah always say, when it itch, you s'posed ta scratch," he said as he playfully pushed her through the door, smiling.

7
FiVe-O On the case

"Dammit, I want action! You can't tell me that someone can get shot in front of a hundred witnesses and no one saw a thing. I want an arrest NOW or you two will be back on foot patrol!"

Deputy Chief Spitz was being unreasonable as usual — always threatening to bump someone down into a lower-paying position.

"We're doing all we can, sir. We do have a few leads that we'll follow up on today," responded Johnson.

"I don't want explanations, Johnson, just results."

"Sir, but ..."

"But nothing, the district attorney is on my back for an arrest and he ain't smilin, so you two better get it in gear, quick."

"Yes sir."

Johnson and Hernandez walked out of Spitz's office to

the transportation section for their service vehicle. Johnson hated Spitz's guts and usually had to work overtime to control his emotions around the runt. He'd like nothing better than to choke the life out of the idiot, and looked forward to the day that bigot would get transferred off the swing-swift detail.

Adam Spitz III was from a long line of cops. His grandfather Adam Sr., dad Adam Jr., and uncle Alan were all lifelong peace officers. Many of his promotions were the direct result of nepotism.

He had the appearance of a bookworm, standing five seven on a measly hundred-and-fifty-pound body. A receding hairline along with bifocals made him seem much older than his forty years.

Coming from a family of racists, Spitz despised the ugly, overgrown Negro. He hated Johnson's black ass and secretly waited for the day Johnson would make a career-ending mistake. Then he'd be the department's poster boy for all other Negroes who had the nerve to choose life as a crime fighter.

Without the gun and badge, Spitz had no spine. He enjoyed the power his current position gave him, especially since it allowed him authority over blacks, Chicanos, and Asians, all of whom he considered inferior.

Growing up in a sheltered lily-white environment, his people skills were poor when it came to dealing with minorities. Spitz hated the fact that due to affirmative action, all those idiots were contaminating the force. Picking up the phone, he called Schiller's Cafe and ordered a meatloaf with mashed potato and gravy dinner.

He always called ahead to order his food so it would be ready for pickup when he arrived. Most of his friends labeled him impatient, but Spitz considered this an asset along with his good planning. Lifting his coat off the rack, he took the short walk to get his meal.

"What's the girl's address?" Johnson asked his partner.

"832 Campbell Street."

"And the other?"

"Right next door."

"You know what keeps eating away at me, Manny?"

"What's that, Nate?"

"Why would they take shoes off a dead man's feet? There's no logic to that." Turning right at 8th and Campbell then pulling over, the two officers headed up the walkway towards unit 832. Doris Adkins and Yvette Mims resided in Campbell Village. Located in the boondocks, the neighborhood's appearance was similar to many of the older projects.

The complex was huge, covering the area from 8th to 10th, Peralta to Campbell. All of the units looked the same on the inside, with the downstairs consisting of small living/dining room combinations along with a kitchen. Upstairs were the beds and bathrooms.

Dope was peddled throughout, and once you entered the plex, if you didn't know your way around, it was very easy to get lost or mugged. Like most places in the vill, if you were unknown, it was better to stay out because strangers were always viewed as undercover cops.

Doris and Yvette had lived next door to each other all their lives and were closer than most sisters. They'd witnessed many fist fights and killings in the hood, but never one from such close range. Yvette and her mom Rosie had spent the entire day at Doris' home trying to help her mother Darlene comfort Doris, who was acting like a zombie.

Like most inner-city teens, the girls considered it a great accomplishment just to graduate from high school. Their immediate plan was to attend Merritt Junior College in order to attain degrees in nursing.

After that they would secure jobs as registered nurses at a local hospital. Considering that they'd both failed chemistry in high school, this would not be an easy journey.

Yvette saw the cops amble up the walkway. "Mama, those are the two pigs from last night! Why can't they just leave us alone?"

"They think you saw somethin, baby," Darlene answered instead of Rosie.

Opening the front door, she stood there waiting for the two officers to reach her porch.

"Excuse me, ma'am, I'm Sargeant Johnson and this is my partner Sargeant Hernandez. We're looking for Doris Adkins." They displayed their badges.

"What do you want with my daughter?"

"We need to ask her a few questions regarding a murder."

"Seems like they told you last night that they don't know nothing."

"Well, sometimes it may seem insignificant, but you never know."

"Okay, I'll let you do your job, come in."

Johnson entered then sat on the loveseat while his partner remained standing. Hernandez made it a rule to always stand inside anyone's home because it kept him alert and ready in case all hell broke loose.

When Hernandez was a rookie responding to a domestic dispute call, the man suddenly turned on him and before he knew it, his face was pummeled into a bloody mess. Hernandez vowed to never again become too cozy while on a case. Of course, he also became the butt of many precinct jokes.

Unlike many project dwellings that the officers had been in over the years, Darlene Adkins' apartment was clean. Her sofa and loveseat were yellow velvet covered in plastic. Brown coffee end tables with square glass inserts were in front of and on the sides of the couch.

The lamps were gold glass at the bottom with the shades also covered in plastic, and the dinette set was an octagon-shaped glass table lined by wood and four cheap-looking chairs. These could be bought anywhere for ninety-nine dollars.

She had a small off-brand microwave, along with a nineteen-inch bargain basement television. Doris aimlessly wandered down the stairs, taking a seat on the sofa next to Yvette.

It was easy to see where Doris got her good looks and stallion frame because Darlene Adkins was phine. A rather young-looking thirty-eight, she wore form-fitting turquoise stretch pants with matching halter top.

Her butt and breasts were both big and looked delicious, along with hair neatly trimmed in a close-cropped style. Darlene would always catch the most elegant bachelors, but once they realized that the only thing she had going was her looks and body, they wouldn't stay around too long. She also begged too much, figuring since she gave up a little tail, the man should volunteer to pay her phone bill or cable.

Yvette's mom Rosie was high yellow with freckles, chubby, and got down with nothing but losers. Every man she met would eventually make a play for Darlene, and she knew when Darlene told her that it was true. It pained her psyche knowing men could be such dogs.

Just as Yvette looked now, Rosie was also once sexy. However, all the years on welfare with nothing to do but sit her rump watching soaps had taken a toll.

Rosie wore black jeans, high heels, and a white blouse. Since today was the first and they'd already cashed their welfare check, she and Darlene wanted five-o to get on with it so they could get ready for girls' night out.

Every month on the first Thursday, Darlene and Rosie treated themselves to a night at Sweet Jimmie's, which was located on the corner of 17th and San Pablo. Jimmie's catered to the older set.

You could always catch a few good blues bands on weekends, be part of the talent contest on Tuesdays, or participate in the Thursday night lip-sync contest, which was televised by Soulbeat.

Darlene received drink after drink from men seeking her company. She would also be on the dance floor all night. Rosie, on the other hand, religiously taped the show

FIVE-O ON THE CASE

(which aired on Friday nights), and although spotting Darlene throughout, she rarely saw herself on tape.

"Okay," Johnson began, "is there anything you can tell me?"

"I don't remember nothing," Doris responded.

Darlene prepared dinner in the kitchen while Hernandez greedily watched her every move. His hormones were on fire as the stoutly built black woman wiggled and jiggled her wares in front of him. Darlene knew he was watching so she put extra emphasis in every move. She enjoyed making a man squirm.

"What did the suspects have on?"

"I don't know."

"Type of car?" Johnson pressed.

"I don't know."

"Have you ever seen them before?"

"No."

"What about the victim?"

"Who, Stoney?"

"Yes, how well did you know the guy?"

"We just used to see him around, I really didn't know him at all."

"Did he say anything?"

"No."

Frustrated and realizing that he wouldn't gather any useful information here, Johnson got up, handing business cards to both Doris and Yvette.

"If you think of anything that might be of help, don't hesitate to call me."

Giving his partner the eye, Johnson thanked Darlene and Rosie, then the two officers walked out.

"Where to now, Nate?" Hernandez inquired.

"Let's go back to the scene of the crime."

"Okay, partner."

. . .

Rolling up to the corner of 14th, they found it booming more than usual. The first day of the month always brought everyone outside. People went about their normal routine as if nothing had happened the night before. Upon seeing five-o, they scattered.

"Look at that," Hernandez stated with disgust, "besides blood stains, you wouldn't know a murder was committed right here last night. Your people are strange, Nate."

"Manny, you go talk with the store owners; I'll question the riff-raff."

"Done."

They exited their vehicle in different directions. Johnson hated the way Hernandez stereotyped blacks. One would think he would have gotten used to it over the years, but it still hit a nerve. He had his own prejudices against Mexicans but would never state them openly to his partner.

Johnson secretly knew it was only a matter of time before he'd have to check Manny on that issue. Whenever that time came, their relationship would forever be destroyed — he knew that also.

While Hernandez tried unsuccessfully to get the store and restaurant owners to talk, Johnson watched the block empty due to the fact five-o was on the set. He knew that many people on the corner had skeleton bones in their closet, and the last person they would deal with would be a cop.

The heat was a monster, with '93 rapidly turning into one of the hottest summers ever. Thinking about his family plans for the Fourth of July, which was only days away, Johnson removed his jacket and plucked the hanky from his pocket.

Wiping his perspiring forehead, he glanced upward, spotting the dangling shoes on the telephone line. "Well I'll be damned," he said to himself. Jumping on the car's radio transmitter, he got central dispatch on the line.

"Dispatch, this is Sargeant Johnson, and I need someone from the phone company to meet me at 14th and Peralta in order to retrieve a pair of sneakers from their line, pronto."

The 911 operator found this request strange but followed instructions to the letter. By the time the phone company employee arrived and retrieved the shoes, a crowd had assembled, curious as to why the cops would ignore shoes on lines in all neighborhoods daily but want this particular pair.

It didn't take long for them to figure out that those shoes belonged to Stoney. Plus, you didn't throw Air Jordans away like that. Johnson instructed the worker to handle the shoes with latex gloves and place them in a plastic zip-lock bag. He and Manny then headed for the crime lab with what they hoped would be their first solid lead.

8
FAMILY IN MOURNING

The drive to Momma's was only ten blocks but seemed like an eternity. She lived on Fruitvale, which was a stone's throw from Jingletown. Next door to her crib sat a halfway house where some of the weirdest characters in the city resided.

Across the street was a mini-market complete with a two-pump island for gasoline. A Mexican-run community center was situated on the opposite corner, equipped with game room, pool table, gymnasium, and kitchen.

Serving as many black teens as Latinos, the center lined up numerous field trips, along with teaching youngsters how to prepare dishes such as spaghetti, fried chicken, tacos, burritos, and enchiladas.

Momma lived in apartment number one, which faced the street. She spent most days peering out her window viewing the madness. Over the years, Mexicans had moved into each vacant unit until Mom was the only remaining black tenant.

We routinely attempted to convince her to relocate, but she always declined. The building had a security gate that never locked properly, and on the few occasions when someone would make certain it was secure, visitors would have to rap on Momma's window, asking her to let them in.

All the Mexicans called her "Mamacita" and she knew each one of them, along with all their kids' names, ages, and birth dates. Mom would cook big meals daily, feeding anyone who was hungry. It was nothing to walk into her home and find tenants or residents from the crazy house eating dinner.

The Mexicans brought her plates of food regularly as thanks for opening the gate for their friends. She would save cigarettes left behind by family or friends so that her people who smoked could have one. Everyone was referred to as "baby," and she always gave hugs freely.

Momma's attire was the same daily. A small woman, she tended to wear thin, colorful house robes with slippers. She owned at least thirty of them, but for Christmas, her birthday, or Mother's Day she would tell you to just buy her a robe because the one she had was getting old.

She could drink with the best and expected you to bring a bottle anytime you set foot in her house. Having outlived three husbands, my dad included, Momma had no plans to wed again.

Taking care of her grandchildren and the neighborhood

kids kept her energy level high. She didn't have teeth and only wore her false ones for special occasions. When she did put them in her mouth, she looked very funny to us.

I parked across the street, went in, and made a beeline to the bathroom, wanting to freshen up. Mom always kept extra toothbrushes for all her grown children.

"Damn, what happened to you?" my sister Rochelle asked.

"I had a little problem."

"Looks like you got yo ass whupped."

"Shut up, girl."

I closed the bathroom door with Rochelle's laughter ringing in my ears. Looking in the mirror, I saw the onion was still there, but it had gotten smaller. Getting myself together quickly, I joined everyone in the living room. The house was full of relatives, kids, and friends.

"Hey, Mom, what happened?" I asked.

"Yo brutha was standin on dat conah and somebody shot 'im."

"What corner, 14th and Peralta?"

"Yeah, dass where he was."

"Do they know who did it?"

"Naw, nobody know nuthin."

Momma wasn't her usual self, because losing a child is the greatest tragedy a parent will face. She had dark circles around her eyes from crying all night. Everyone was trying to comfort her.

"Pearlie Mae, it's gone be all right. God don't make mistakes," Rochelle stated.

Mom was called Pearlie Mae by everyone except me. Looking weak and very old, she asked, "Rainbow, what happened to yo face?"

"I had a fight! Where is the body?"

"Da coroner got it."

"Anybody call Charles?"

"Not yet."

I picked up the phone and called my job, then Williams Funerals. When the receptionist answered, I asked to speak with Charles Williams. Every time someone in my family passed away, this outfit handled the arrangements. Charles Williams, the owner, looked no older than forty, but his company provided excellent, traditional-style service. The thing I liked most was that Charles would come to your house, saving you the trouble of going to the funeral home.

"Williams Funeral Home, Charles speaking."

"Charles, this is Rainbow, Pearlie Mae's son."

"How you doing, Rainbow?"

"Not too good. My brother Ricky's been murdered."

"Your family has my deepest sympathy. What do you need?"

"First, I need you to go get the body."

"Who has it, the coroner?"

"Yes."

"Consider it done. You know, I should have been called immediately to pick up the body. It would have saved you the fee the county charges for the service."

"I know, but all that's water under the bridge."

"Will you be coming in?"

"No, we were hoping you could come here — you know how Momma is."

"Okay, let me check my schedule." After a minute Charles returned on the line. "Rainbow, I can be there at twelve-thirty."

"That's fine, we'll see you then."

"Stay strong, bro."

"Later, Charles."

I hung up and relayed the information to Rochelle, my two brothers Rodney and Rufus, along with their spouses, Ricky's wife Sabrina, Momma, and the kids.

"When do you want the funeral, Mom?"

"I'ont know, baby, when do you thank?"

"I think we should have the wake Sunday night and the funeral Monday."

"That's fine, baby — I want you to handle all dis fo me."

"I'll handle it, Mom. Where's the insurance policy?"

"It's in my bedroom, top drawer of the nightstand."

Pearlie Mae had seventy-five-hundred-dollar insurance policies on all her children. She religiously paid the premiums on the first of the month with part of her disability check. Joining everyone in the living room, policy in hand, I gave it to her.

"Give this to Charles, and let him deal with the insurance company."

"Okay, baby."

"I'll be back later."

"Where you goin?"

"I got a few things I need to do. I'll be back."

It's something about death that brings out the worst in families, especially when there's an insurance policy involved. Everyone seems to think there will be money left over, when it costs almost seventy-five hundred to give a loved one a proper burial. My siblings were no different — they looked like vultures circling wounded prey.

Rochelle was the greediest, since she never had anything except a hard time. Five kids by three different losers, welfare and Section 8 her entire adult life, she felt as though the world owed her something. Big as a house from having all those kids, she woke up and went to bed drinking. She would look to skim on the price of the entire funeral, calculating how much money was left, and how much her "cut" would be, being Ricky's sister and all.

We never had a typical brother-sister relationship, because her logic was stuck on stupid. Viewing the monthly AFDC checks as her money, she allowed her kids to walk around nasty, dirty, and hungry. When I would tell her that the money should be used for the children, she'd get fighting mad, telling me in no uncertain terms to mind my own business.

I couldn't see how she could be dressed nice every day but let her kids look so pitiful. She displayed no signs of the pain you'd think someone had for losing a brother. Her explanation was that she was grieving in her own way. What that was, nobody knew because she kept tilting the bottle while talking crazy.

Maxine was reaching for the policy before Momma

could even take it out of the plastic holder. Maxine was my older brother Rufus' wife, and she considered herself smarter than everyone she knew, especially the in-laws. Working as a supervisor for A.C. Transit bus company, she was in the habit of considering herself above most people. The girl was snobbish.

She had a pretty decent frame and also had Rufus pussy-whipped. He couldn't control her and would get clowned in a minute if he tried. I really didn't care for her, because a few of my homeboys told me she was giving up booty on a regular basis at work.

She was so used to giving orders at her job that it carried over into her personal life. Bossing Rufus around daily only helped to swell her ego. Maxine didn't have many friends, and her employees hated her guts. Unlike Rochelle, she didn't want money, only to show how much intelligence she possessed.

Rodney observed it all with a look of disgust. He was the oldest and the biggest. Six three and built like a rock, he was soft-spoken and generous. He worked in construction as a carpenter and coached Little League baseball in his spare time.

Rod was never too busy for kids, taking them bowling, fishing, to movies — he'd spend every Saturday doing things with other folks' children. His wife Elaine was busy cooking breakfast today so that the youngsters could eat.

Elaine worked as an Executive Secretary for the State of California. Those two made a very nice couple and they really loved each other. They had been married for twenty years but together since middle school. They knew each

other like a book, often giving the eye and nodding, knowing what the other was thinking without saying a word.

Sabrina just sat there crying while anyone close
attempted to console her. Ricky's wife Sabrina was a
snake, as venomous as they come. She stayed with him
because he supplied her with cash and dope. They both
cheated on each other, so there wasn't that much love in
their relationship.

He stayed with her because of the children, who Sabrina
would drop off all over town. She spent her days riding
around in the '78 Seville Ricky bought for her. If she
wasn't visiting folks, she was looking for Rick. Once she
found him, they'd argue and call each other every dirty
name in the book. Those two put on a daily show for the
entire corner to see.

Giving Momma a hug and kiss on the cheek, I bounced.
Hopping in Bertha, I headed up Fruitvale to the MacArthur
Freeway, hooked a left onto 580, and drove downtown.
Making a right on 14th, I cruised into the boondocks.

· · ·

Pulling up in front of the liquor store at 14th and Peralta,
I parked and got out. I went in the store, bought a fifth of
brandy, bottle of cola, small bag of ice, and two cups.
Walking to the corner of 13th, I headed up to Luther's
house. He was sitting in his usual chair on the porch.

Luther Miller was the neighborhood alcoholic. His
house was similar to all the rest, a beat-up Victorian needing more improvements than he would ever be able to
afford. It was also the community house. As long as you

brought him something to drink, you could use his place.

Luther was five foot six and weighed one hundred and forty pounds. He had skinny legs, a big beer belly, and puffy face from years of drinking liquor. Alcohol was his breakfast, lunch, and dinner.

Formerly married with a decent job working as a circulation driver for the daily paper, Luther let his addiction to alcohol get out of control, which led his wife to have an affair. She fell in love, packed up the kids, and cut out. Luther was devastated, started drinking day and night, and eventually lost his job and self-esteem.

Ricky and the rest of the dealers would package up dope, bring girls in and have sex, shoot dice, or just sit in the kitchen eating lunch and counting money. As long as they gave Luther fresh liquor and a few dollars, he'd sit on his porch telling anybody's business or lying about how great he used to be.

"Whatup Lou?"

"Rainbow, my man, ain't seen you in a long time. Man, I'm sorry bout what happened to Stoney, man."

"Thanks, Luther."

I handed him the bag of goodies, which his eyes had been glued on since my arrival. Luther poured himself a full-cup shot of brandy straight, while I fixed a very weak one that was ninety percent soda.

"Luther, I need to know what you saw."

"Man, I didn't see nuthin, man."

"Lou, you always on this porch seeing everything, you had to see something."

"Man, I'm sorry bout yo brother, you know I liked

Stoney — he always took good care of me. If I'da saw somethin I'd tell you."

Deciding to let Luther absorb more liquor before continuing, I changed the subject.

"What are you doing for the Fourth?"

"Sunday? I ain't got no plans — hoping somebody brang me a plate of bar-b-que!"

"I met this new honey, so I'll probably see if we gonna hook up; if not, I'll be with family."

Luther had refilled twice and was ready to shoot off at the mouth.

"Man, you shoulda seen the way these people were scattering — that fool was shootin at anythang that moved."

"It was crazy, huh, Lou?"

"Crazy ain't the word, those fools is psycho. I knew something was wrong the minute they pulled up."

"You saw them?"

"Rainbow, if it wasn't yo brother they shot, I wouldn't tell you."

"I know, man, you and Ricky was tight, huh?"

"Yeah, we was tight. Stoney could always depend on me. Look, you keep dis under yo hat."

Leaning over towards me and speaking in a hushed tone, Luther gave up game.

"The car they was ridin in belong to Spodie. I don't know if he was with 'em, but I know that was one of his cars."

"You talkin about fat Spodie who fixes cars?"

"Yep."

"Live with his momma in Dogtown?"

"I don't know bout all that, just know what I see, and I saw his car pick up the two people shootin."

"Two people? The police only mentioned one."

"Well, you know how the police always ass-backwards. There was two of them fools. One did the shootin while the other did the stealin."

"How many more of 'em was it, Lou?"

"There was two moe in the car."

"Hey Luther, look, I'd love to sit here and shoot the shit with you, but I gotta run, man — need to get these arrangements made for Stoney's funeral."

"Okay, blood, let me know when the funeral gone be."

"Alright."

I left Luther on his porch with his booze. He'd have enough to last until the mailman arrived, which would be soon. The main post office was located on Seventh Street, so all the west-side people got their mail first thing in the morning.

There were already porches full of folks waiting on their monthly handout. Seeing this scene always made my mind think of the phrase "porch monkeys," by which whites had so hatefully referred to blacks down south.

Getting out of Dodge, I went downtown and parked in City Center garage. I took the escalator upstairs and walked to the tuxedo shop. One-day rentals were sixty-five dollars, so after they measured me, I paid them three hundred and ninety dollars and gave the names of the five other pallbearers who would be coming in to get fitted.

One thing about Stoney was his haberdashery. The boy

dressed every day, so for his funeral it was only fitting that we all looked good, too. I didn't want six differently styled black suits worn by my brother's pallbearers. Also, with all of us dressed identical, we'd be fly.

Leaving the store, I went across the walkway for a cup of coffee. Ordering a large cup of french roast, I grabbed a seat outside, bought a paper, and attempted to read. Changing my mind and deciding to people-watch instead, I sat there tripping off the working class.

City Center is a collection of stores, restaurants, and offices based in the heart of downtown. Like everything else downtown, on weekends it resembles a ghost town. During the week, however, it bustles with activity.

The stores make most of their money from office workers. Located right across the street is the Federal Building, a big yellow monstrosity with twin towers that mirror one another. The entrance to the building is in the center, and whether you want to go to the north or south tower, you have to pass through metal detectors. The building houses mostly Internal Revenue employees.

City Hall down the street, along with three other buildings housing city employees, represents another thousand or more customers daily to the center. You also have numerous private company staff, passersby, and people doing business in the area. If downtown had had a nightlife, City Center would have blossomed.

Finishing my coffee and taking the escalator back down to the garage, I got in Bertha and headed home. On the way my pager went off. It was Cassandra. Any other time after the night we had, I would have gotten off at the first exit and called her immediately, but since I had some serious questions to ask, the comforts of home would be a better place to talk. Before I got to the house, she had beeped again.

Parking on the street, I checked the mailbox then went in the front door. Iceberg greeted me with his usual excitement, tail wagging and tongue hanging out. I fixed him some lunch along with a fresh bowl of water, then sat down and turned on "Mason."

Mason is my 386 clone computer which I use to write lyrics, college homework, and personal papers, or just kill time playing solitaire. After taking a minute to gather my thoughts, I picked up the phone and called Cassandra.

"Hello."

"Hi Cassandra, this is Rainbow."

"Hey baby, I've been thinking about you all morning. I tried calling, but I guess you went to work. I took the day off."

"Check this out, I need to have a serious conversation with you, so you think we can get together later?"

"That's fine — is everything alright?"

"Not really. My brother was murdered last night." After a long silence, Cassandra spoke. "Do you need me for anything?" she said with alarm.

"No, I got it under control, but I still need to talk to you later."

"Rainbow, now you're scaring me — what is it?"

"Listen, I'll be free at about six o'clock."

"Stay where you are, I'm on my way." She hung up before I could say another word.

Going from room to room, I straightened up the house

so it would be clean when Cassandra arrived. When I saw her drive up, I waited at the door. She walked up the steps and gave me a kiss, her Chloe perfume going straight to my nostrils and brain as I inhaled the fragrance.

She hugged me so tight that our bodies felt like one. Whatever I intended to say would have to wait because her body eliminated all questions. Leading her into my home, I gave her a tour of the place. Noticing that she was afraid of Iceberg, I sent him to the backyard.

"What has you so worried, baby?" she asked with concern.

"Well, when I left your house last night, some fool tried to jump me."

"What? Who?"

"I don't know him, but he did warn me to stay away from you."

"What did he look like?"

"It was too dark to tell, but he did have an ugly woman and a beat-up Caddy."

"Buckey and Violet."

"Who?" I asked.

"Baby, it had to be Buckey and Violet — they are the only people I know who fit that description and would do such a thing."

"Who are they?"

"Buckey is my ex-husband Calvin's little brother, Violet is his woman. Calvin is in prison for beating me up. We broke up before he went to jail, but he won't accept it. Every man I've met in the last six months has been run off by Buckey."

"How did they know we were together?"

"I don't know. The only thing I can think of is Nadine probably told them, that bitch."

"Who, may I ask, is Nadine?"

"She's my neighbor. I think Buckey pays her to watch me."

"So that's why you choose not to date? Because they have you scared?"

"I'm not afraid of them, I just don't want you to get hurt on account of me."

"Look, I can handle that fool. Where do they live?"

"They stay on the west side — Chestnut Street, across from the Acorn."

As she talked, she continually stroked my face. I held her in my arms and she began crying softly. She had on a cherry-colored dress with matching pumps and purse. We embraced, which caused my manhood to swell and rise. After leading her to my bedroom, we both stripped down and made passionate love. The sounds of our bodies slapping together was music to my ears.

"Rainbow, no one has ever made me feel the way you do."

"Tell me the full scoop of you and your ex-husband's break-up."

"He wouldn't work, gave me no respect, and cheated on me."

"How long had you been together?"

"We were together for ten years, married seven. At first it was cool, but once he got deep into his womanizing, he didn't ring my bell anymore, spreading it around too thin, I guess. I mean, after being together for so long, the sex got plain. Most couples have this problem but when the love is there, you find ways to work it out, to have variety in your lovemaking. All I got was a wham, bam, thank you ma'am. It got to the point where he would take me even though I was dry and not ready to be taken. I was miserable."

"Do you think you played a part in it?"

"It depends on how you look at it. I mean, if you call getting burned out on being faithful, cooking, cleaning, working, and raising the kids, while my man is out partying and screwing anything in sight as me playing a part, then I guess I did."

"Come on, let's take a shower."

We showered together, with her soaping my back then me returning the favor. Taking turns drying each other off, we dressed then she followed me back to Mason, where I began writing my brother's obituary. After about thirty minutes I was satisfied with my work. Cassandra thought it was nice, too. I printed out a copy, then asked, "What do you have planned for today?"

"I thought I was going to spend it with you."

"Well, let's go."

I took the short ride to Pearlie Mae's and we went in. Everyone was still there, with Charles showing them different models of caskets.

"Momma, everybody, this is Cassandra."

"Hi baby, it's so nice to meet you," Momma said, rising to give Cassandra a hug.

I introduced her to all my people one by one. I would tell her about them later. I told Rufus and Rodney about their appointments with the tuxedo shop to be fitted, and they both seemed pleased. Passing around the obituary, they all read it and approved before giving it to Charles. My mother asked Charles to read it to her, which he did with the eloquence of a gospel minister.

OBITUARY

Ricky Dwayne Jordan entered this life on July 12, 1966, born to his proud parents Horace and Pearlie Mae Jordan. Accepting Christ at an early age, he became a member of True Guidance Baptist Church of Richmond, California.

"Stoney," as he was affectionately called by family and friends, had a great love of life. Excelling in athletics, he graduated from John C. Fremont High School in Oaktown, attended U.C. Berkeley on a football scholarship, and starred until suffering a career-ending knee injury.

Later he met and married the love of his life, Sabrina Morgan. This union lasted until his untimely death and produced two offspring. Stoney was loved by all and was a man of his word. He will be sorely missed.

He leaves to celebrate his life, his wife Sabrina Denise Jordan; two sons, Mitchell D'Andre and Michael Dwayne Jordan; his mother Pearlie Mae Cannon; one sister, Rochelle Marie Jordan; three brothers, Rodney Antonio, Rufus Dejuan, and Reggie Alexander Jordan, and two sisters-in-law Maxine and Elaine Jordan, all of Oaktown.

Stoney also leaves a host of nieces, nephews, aunts, uncles, cousins, and friends.

By the time Charles finished reading, Pearlie Mae had tears streaming down her cheeks. We put the final touches on the arrangements and Charles left. On his way out he told me that the insurance had been approved and advised me to get to Rolling Hills and make burial arrangements. I took Cassandra's hand, gave Momma a kiss, then we bounced.

The drive to the cemetery was free of traffic, which was a relief. It seemed like Cal Trans was always building something on I-80, but today even the MacArthur Maze was only lightly congested. We got there in about thirty minutes.

Rolling Hills is a classic burial ground with hills and valleys of neatly manicured grass. Construction is commonplace. They always create more room for the dead. One thing they understand that most people hate to face is the fact we'll all die eventually.

The cemetery is located in the Hilltop neighborhood of Richmond. Everyone we knew had been buried there. Upon entering the business office, we found that they were expecting me. I decided on a plot in the Garden of Eden, filled out the paperwork, visited a few of my people's graves, then we headed back to Oaktown.

Cassandra was impressed by the way I was handling it all, but she was at a loss for words. Considering the circumstance, it was understandable. She held my hand the entire way, removing hers only when I had to change lanes.

We got back to Oaktown, where I exited at 27th Street. Going into Dogtown, I went to fat Spodie's house. Leaving Cassandra in the car, I went to the garage in back, where I figured he'd be since he was a mechanic. A set of eyes watched my every move, but I was oblivious. Since the door was already open, I went in.

Wannabe Kingpin

Buckey woke to the noise of the garbage trucks making their weekly pick-ups. Violet lay peacefully asleep butt-naked. They always slept in the nude and engaged in sex nightly. Watching her large breasts rising and falling upon each breath, Buckey became aroused instantly.

Spreading her legs apart, he forced his way in then began slamming his meat into her with reckless abandon. Violet's body woke up before her mind. She loved waking up with him inside pumping furiously.

The harder his thrusts, the more thoroughly she enjoyed it. Sex to Violet was her man making it hurt. She'd scratch his back and thrash her head from side to side while humping and screaming loudly. This madness only excited him more, causing him to spread her cheeks while attempting to push his bone through her.

Turning her over on her belly, he hit it doggie style, sending waves of pleasure through her body. Their style of lovemaking could only be classified as animalistic lust. Be it oral, anal, or sucking on toes, it didn't matter because by the time they were done, each would be totally spent.

Every ounce of energy was used to satisfy the other. Buckey exploded inside Violet, with the heat from his liquid triggering her own orgasm. They both sprawled on the bed gasping for air. Pulling out, he got up and put on the same dirty clothes from the day before.

"Where you goin, baby?" she asked as juice bubbled out of her slit.

"Goin ta sell mah dope."

"Once I broke it all down and packaged it up, you had seven thousand dollars' worth."

"Ah no, we gone be livin large in a minute, shidd."

"Ooh baby, that sounds good to me. I'm gonna buy me a couple of outfits today — you want me to pick you up anything?"

"Yeah, get me some moe jeans, a sweatsuit, an a pair of kicks."

"Okay, baby."

Violet rolled over and went back to sleep as Buckey walked out the door. He never brushed his teeth or washed his face, so to him facing the world dirty and stinking was normal. Violet didn't care about his filth because she wasn't the most sanitary person in the world, either.

Deciding it would be safer to walk, Buckey crossed the street and took a shortcut through the Acorn. Reappearing at Eighth and Market, he went to Mickey D's and bought a sausage, egg, and pancake breakfast.

The parking lot was full, with the line outside the

check-cashing center already snaking around the corner. The place wouldn't open for another half hour, but the early birds already had their worm.

Acorn Center was a joke. Along with the burger joint was a Chinese take-out, laundromat, check-cashing center, and supermarket. The market was an oversized corner store whose ownership changed on a regular basis. Their prices were ridiculous, and shoppers along with employees stole merchandise like it was the thing to do. The thefts only caused the outrageous prices to soar through the roof.

If west-side residents wanted to pay reasonable prices, they had to shop in another part of town. Across from the center was a service station complete with car wash facilities. The opposite corner housed a construction company business office.

Directly across the street sat the "Highrises" alongside "Da Mo'houses." The Highrises were an apartment complex eleven stories high blended with working class, seniors, and welfare cases. Although it was called the Highrises, the place really wasn't that tall.

Buckey completed his meal then went outside. Seeing many familiar faces, he approached a dude he knew named Randy.

"Randog, wuzup fool?"

"Buckey Jones, what's happenin, baby?"

"Aw, it ain't shit, man, what you doin down heah?"

"Buck, I'm doin what all the fly niggahs do — waitin on mah bitch ta cash that check, what clse?" They both laughed and shook hands.

"Look dog, ah want y'all ta know det ah got da dope."

Buckey broke him off a huge piece of rock then went to occupy a spot at the base of a lamp post. Just as he predicted, Randy immediately started bragging to everyone in line about his boy Buckey and the good-ass dope he had.

Proudly displaying his rock for all to see, Randy informed folks that they would have to place their orders through him. His woman saw what he was up to and began searching around for any of her girlfriends who had a car. She knew if he smoked that rock before she got her scrill, he would take it and blow it all with that horse-looking creep he was worshipping.

Buckey didn't know Randy Evans that well, but did see him all the time chasing welfare women with low self-esteem. Always talking loud trying to impress, Randy was well-known to the ladies as a fake who didn't have shit. Word through the female grapevine had it that the boy had a big bone, but that was all. However, for many man-starved women that was more than enough.

The minute checks were cashed, Buckey was open for business. One by one people spent their long-awaited money on the poison he supplied. The clock struck eleven and he'd already made a thousand dollars along with three hundred in food stamps.

Buckey thought he was the man because in the ghetto if you had dope for sale, you had clout. The dope fiends made you feel that way. Randy's woman snuck away when he wasn't looking, but he didn't care. Buckey had promised him a hundred-dollar commission plus a hundred in rocks if he stayed and brought customers. He knew once

Randy smoked the rocks, he'd bring the money right back. Violet came rolling through in their lemon with a few chicken-head homegirls. She wore an orange summer dress cut low with a split down the side.

Buckey went to the driver-side window, excitedly telling her how much money he'd made. Next, he gave her a wad of cash along with instructions to hide it with the rest of his stash. Giving her a kiss, he returned to his spot and watched her drive off.

Buckey sat there hour after hour getting paid. When he needed more dope, he'd get a ride to the crib from a return customer, paying them a twenty-dollar rock for their services.

Violet returned at three o'clock, and since business had slowed to a crawl, Buckey got in. Handing Randy a generous bonus, Buckey informed him where he would be for the next several hours. He also promised him a job selling rocks as long as he didn't cross him.

"Take me ta Wino Park," he told his woman.

"You wanna eat first?" she asked.

"Naw, I'mo make dis money foe dese foos spinit wif somebody else."

"Well, I'm going ta eat. I'll brang you somethin back, okay?"

"Dat'll work."

Violet drove to the park grinning while Buckey talked like a kingpin. Getting out, he kissed her on the lips and took off in the direction of the crowd.

"I'll be back in a little while with yo food, baby," she said.

Buckey didn't hear her because he was too busy making it known that he had rocks for sale. Lafayette Square was situated downtown, spanning one square city block surrounded by 10th, 11th, Jefferson, and Martin Luther King.

Referred to as "Wino Park" or "Old Man's Park," it consisted of patches of grass, benches, and walkways. At the edge of the park was a shed housing gardening equipment. Restrooms sandwiched the shed, and once you entered, it was at your own risk.

Dope fiends shooting heroin, freebasing, or having sex took place continuously. Someone would come in and take a crap, remove their shirt or underwear to wipe their behind, then go back outside as if nothing was strange about what they'd just done.

The water faucet was pyramid-shaped with a bronze dedication plaque engraved on the facade. It stayed full of dirt and never worked. Homeless people slept on the grass or benches with their lifelong possessions nearby in shopping carts.

Mother Wright came on Wednesdays, Saturdays, and Sundays, giving out free meals and clothing to whoever needed them. Her only requirement was that they first clean the park, use no profanity, and participate in prayer. She was a godsend because for many park dwellers this would be their only solid meal for days. They would also have leftovers for an additional day or two.

The center of activity was the domino table, where crowds gathered to watch excellently played domino games. To the average person rolling by, that's all they'd see. What they missed were the dice games right next to the domino table.

It was a well-known fact throughout the city that big-money crap games were at Wino Park. Gamblers arrived from every hood seeking to increase their bank. Unlike most neighborhood games where you usually had to break every last player, here if you won a grand and wanted to quit, you could because someone else was always waiting to assume your spot. Today Buckey avoided the game — he was making money a different way.

"Look, ah wont all da foos ta know ah got da dope and ah take cash, food stamps, or quality merchandise," he boasted.

Buckey opened shop and immediately raked in cash, jewelry, clothes, and household appliances. Word was out that Buckey had the shit.

One hour later Violet arrived with their dinners from Everett & Jones. With a reputation for the best homemade sauce in the city, this eatery had lots of regular customers, and Violet was one of them. She and Buckey sat at a bench eating their ribs and links while fiends continually interrupted to buy drugs.

Each time it happened, Buckey gave Violet a knowing look, as if to say, "I told you so." She was impressed by the attention her man received, because normally most people stayed as far away from Buckey as they could get. Now they freely flocked to him.

Within an hour he'd sold out again, so he and Violet hopped in their bucket and headed back to the pigsty they called home. Once they entered, Violet slipped out of her dress and grabbed two beers from the fridge, handing Buckey one while parading around the house in her panties and high heels.

To be so ugly in the face, Violet possessed a beautiful body, and those big melons always turned Buckey on. He threw her down roughly on the dirty carpet, and they had sex right then and there.

Buckey was so exhausted from the last two days of sex and violence that he slept until Friday morning. Violet spent the evening counting scrill while dreaming of how wealthy they would become. She also attempted to clean up but did not succeed.

Both Earl and Slack came over that evening, but seeing Buckey passed out on the living room floor barely covered by a blanket, they told Violet that they would return tomorrow.

10
THE
INTERROGATION

Arriving back at the station, Johnson and Hernandez took the Air Jordans to the crime lab in order to be tagged and dusted for prints. Returning to their desks, they wrote reports of the afternoon's activities. Once that was completed they walked one block over for dinner.

On most nights they dined at Mexicali Rose, where the food was good, ambiance exquisite, and the place always packed with cops, their environment. Hernandez ordered his meals in Spanish, trying to show his heritage. Johnson, however, was never impressed.

The exterior was painted pink and the interior decorated Spanish style, with a bar and dining area. The place was always dimly lit, with Mexican or black music softly playing on the twenty-five-cents jukebox.

Hernandez ordered an enchilada plate while Johnson

requested a super burrito a la carte. They ate in silence, each man's mind absorbed in his own thoughts. When they were done they went back to work.

There was a message waiting, instructing them to go to the crime lab. There the techs informed them that a pair of prints was lifted from the shoes. The tech on duty was a Chinese guy named Wah Woon Chang, but he preferred to be called Jimmy.

"What you got, Jimmy?" Hernandez asked.

"I lifted a set of prints off the sneakers and ran them through the computer."

"Did you get a match?"

"I sure did — the name is James McKnight, alias Spodie Dupree."

"What else do you know about him?"

"He's a small-time mechanic, has several old cars registered through Motor Vehicles, and usually hangs out at the rec center across the street from his house."

"You got an address?"

"Yes, 3105 Union Street."

"Does he have a rap sheet, Jimmy?" asked Johnson.

"One DUI conviction, plus a few parking tickets and a citation from the city to clean up his yard."

"Thanks, Jimmy," they said simultaneously.

"You bet," he responded.

Buckey and Earl had both used gloves while handling the sneakers, but Spodie placed them under the seat using his bare hands. As Buckey had predicted, Spodie did something stupid, bringing the cops right to his door.

Johnson and Hernandez entered Spitz's office. As they

84

did so, Spitz threw his legs off the desk and tried to make it appear as though he were rifling through papers. They all knew he was napping but no one said so.

"Well, boys, any new developments?"

"Boss, we got a lead on a suspect," Johnson stated.

"Go on."

"Suspect's name is James McKnight, alias Spodie Dupree. His fingerprints were on the shoes. Jimmy ran a check on the guy but came up empty. However, we do have an address."

"Well, what are you waiting for? Bring his ass in for questioning."

Johnson and Hernandez both walked out pissed. They were in a catch-twenty-two. If they didn't keep Spitz informed, he'd chew them out, but when they did let him know what was happening, he'd talk to them as if they were stupid. As the door shut, Spitz's shoes were once again on the desk.

Getting in their service vehicle, they headed for Spodie's house. On the way a call came over the transmitter about a prowler, and the address given was Spodie's. Hernandez radioed that he and Johnson were headed to that location but would like backup on the scene.

Johnson and Hernandez arrived in two minutes flat, and as they did an elderly woman came over to the car. She had on a blue and white flowered housedress, slippers, and a scarf tied crookedly on her head.

Cassandra watched intently as the woman pointed to where I had just entered. The officers drew their revolvers and surrounded the garage. Cassandra tried to tell police who I was, but they were having none of that. They just stated, "Step back, ma'am."

I went inside the garage, and the first thing I saw was fat Spodie sprawled out in a puddle of blood on the floor. It was obvious he'd been dead for a while because rigor mortis had set in and the stench was awful.

Glancing around, I saw signs of a struggle. Spodie's hand tightly gripped a tire iron. Next to his body lay a solitary latex condom which obviously had been used. This caused me to think that maybe he had gotten caught up in a love triangle that could have resulted in his death.

One thing was certain, he was dead. I went to take a step, nearly breaking my neck over a baseball bat. Not paying attention to what I was doing, I picked it up then noticed it was soaked with blood and the handle missing.

"Freeze, this is the police."

As I turned around slowly, my eyes gazed squarely down the barrel of a semi-automatic. A big black dude and little short Mexican had their guns trained on my dome.

"Man, put the gun away, I just got here."

"Drop the bat slowly, then put your hands up," the black guy said.

"Okay, I'm gonna put the bat down, but I didn't do this."

"Look son, don't make me have to shoot you. Now put the weapon down slowly, keep your hands up high, and drop to your knees."

I did as instructed then they bum-rushed me, slamming me down violently in a puddle of blood. I felt a knee on my neck applying unnecessary pressure. They handcuffed me, then the Mexican read me my rights.

"You have the right to remain silent, anything you say can and will be used against you in a court of law. You have the right to an attorney. . . . "

"Man, what's the charge?" I blurted out.

"You're under arrest for suspicion of murder."

"What? Man, I told you I just got here — I ain't had time to kill nobody."

They half led, half dragged me to a squad car. My shirt was bloody from being thrown to the floor, so I looked guilty as hell. The crowd assembled was already stating as a matter of fact, "He killed Spodic."

Tears freely streamed down Cassandra's face as she watched them shove me inside the back of the black and white. People walked by, peering in at me as if I were on display at a museum. An old lady wandered over, looking at me with disgust. I put my head down, not wanting to face her.

Motioning Cassandra to the squad car with head movements, I yelled to her to go tell my family what went down, then go home and wait for my call. She got in Bertha and sped off as the uniformed officers took me to the station.

Upon arriving at headquarters, they led me through a maze of locked steel doors to the booking area. There they finally uncuffed me. My wrists displayed the indentations of the cuffs. Next they took my wallet and gold, and gave me a choice of letting them take the metal taps off my shoes or going barefoot. I chose to let them take the taps.

They took mug shot photos and fingerprints, then instructed me to pull down my pants and spread my ass cheeks so they could inspect my booty hole. After the desk officers finished the booking process, I was led to a holding cell and shoved inside.

The holding cell was small but had at least twenty prisoners inside. It reeked of funk, and gnats flying around were clearly visible. There was a phone on the wall with a long line of waiting inmates, but all calls had to be collect.

People slept on benches or the dirty floor, and many held conversations. The misfits were obvious, due to the fact that they looked like they didn't belong there. These were the ones arrested for stupid crimes like drunk driving or attempting to solicit a prostitute.

Liquor played a major part in most of these fools' cases. I sat in a daze, peeping out all my cellmates, who were arrested for everything from petty theft to spousal abuse to warrants.

The officers in the control booth kept the PA system turned up loud, so by the time I arrived, everyone knew I was arrested for murder. This resulted in them maintaining their distance, not knowing it wasn't true but respecting me as a dangerous individual. Once the phone line cleared, I called Pearlie Mae.

"Hello."

"Hey Mom, it's me."

"What happened to you?"

"Nothing happened to me."

"Rainbow, if nuthin happened, why you in jail? Dat girl say da police think you kilt somebody."

"Momma, listen, I didn't do it — where's Cassandra anyway?"

"She left, say you tole her ta go home and wait."

"Yeah, that's what I asked her to do. Look, Momma, I'm alright and I didn't do it, so tell everybody that I should be released by tomorrow."

"Awight, I love you, baby."

"I love you too, Momma, and I'll see you later."

"Okay, bye bye."

I hung up then collect-called Cassandra — she answered on the first ring.

"Hello."

"Hey baby, it's me."

"Rainbow, you alright?"

"I'm cool, but you know I was just in the wrong place at the wrong time, right?"

"Baby, I know. What you want me to do?"

"Well, ain't really nothing you can do but wait. They won't complete the booking process until about eight hours from now, so that means no bail amount will be set. For what they're charging me with, we can't afford it anyway."

"Ooh baby, I'm so sorry."

"Sorry for what?"

"You know that dude who was dead?"

"Yeah, fat Spodie."

"He hangs out with Buckey and Violet, be fixin cars for them and ridin them around."

"So all them fools probably had something to do with Ricky's murder. This shit's getting more complicated by the minute."

"Why you say that?"

"Because Luther had no doubts that the getaway car belonged to Spodie, plus there were four people involved and now one of them is dead."

I spoke barely above a whisper because in such a crowded cell every word is heard by someone. Just as I was getting into our conversation, the jailer along with two correction officers called my name.

"Okay, baby, I gotta go, they're calling me."

"Rainbow?"

"Yeah baby?"

"Call and let me know what's going on?"

"Okay, gotta go."

I hung up and was escorted to the second floor homicide office. They removed the cuffs and nudged me into an interrogation room. Waiting for me were the black and Mexican pigs wearing their outdated suits. Instructing me to sit at the table, they began their interrogation, with the black guy going first.

"Okay, Jordan, I'm Johnson; this is my partner Hernandez. We have some questions to ask you, and the quicker you tell us what you know, the better off you'll be. Now here's the way we see it: you found out McKnight had something to do with your brother's murder yesterday, so you killed him in order to get revenge. We figure you know who else was in on it, and you'll go after them too. We don't want you playing vigilante and taking the law into your own hands, so just leave that to us and tell us what you know."

I stared blankly at them.

"Why did you kill McKnight?"

"I didn't kill him. He was dead when I got there."

"How did you get those bruises on your face?"

"Someone jumped me as I left my girlfriend's house last night."

"Look Jordan, you were holding the murder weapon, you knew he had something to do with your brother's death, and you have bruises on your face from the struggle. We got you and you know it, so you'd better start cooperating with us or we can make it very hard on you."

"Man, I told you I didn't do it — that dude had been dead for a long time. I just got there."

"Where were you for the last twenty-four hours?"

"Last night I was with Cassandra Jones, my new girlfriend; today I've been at my mother's house and making plans for my brother's funeral."

We went back and forth like that for the next three hours. One time it would be Johnson, the next Hernandez. One would try to be mean, the other nice. I missed dinner because of these two clowns.

Something wasn't right about my being arrested, and they seemed to know I didn't do it. Hernandez had let it slip that the old lady called about the prowler after she saw me. I pretended not to notice, but somehow they knew I didn't kill Spodie. This time they both walked out.

"Manny, did you hear from the coroner?" Johnson asked his partner.

"Yes, he places time of death between two and three a.m."

"Jordan didn't know about his brother's murder until seven."

"Looks like we'll have to let him go, Nate."

"I know, but I have a feeling this guy knows more than what he's telling us."

"What makes you feel that way?"

"He's too cool — anybody facing a murder rap wouldn't sit there all calm like this guy. He already knows we can't pin it on him, and I get the feeling he ain't gonna talk."

"So what's our next move?"

"We put a tail on him, follow him everywhere he goes."

Johnson and Hernandez came back into the interrogation room and made more small talk with me, but I knew they had nothing. It was only a matter of time before they had to let me go. After about ten minutes the jailer returned and led me to the bullpen.

The bullpen was a huge room housing maybe fifty inmates. There were fifteen sets of bunk beds, which were cold steel with a thin filthy mattress on top. Everything was bolted down including picnic-type metal benches, a twenty-five-inch television set, and three phones on the wall.

There were three shower stalls and four toilets behind a plate-glass window facing the room, so if you wanted to shower or shit, everyone could watch if they chose to do so. Simple domino games would sometimes result in extreme violence, and if you got into a rumble, no one would intervene, so you had to kick ass or get yours kicked. The officers monitoring activity on video screens didn't come in while fists were flying.

Since there were not enough beds, two people shared a spot if they were acquaintances. One would be at the head, the other the foot. Misfits sat at tables or on the floor. Being a "murderer," I had a bed all to myself. Everybody ran their mouth, talking about everything from what they're down for, how it went down, what the police did, who they're gonna get, how much money was involved, or whatever they knew about anybody else's business.

Many people get busted behind jailhouse gossip, unaware that the police sit in their monitoring booth with the speaker system turned up. Brothers get to bragging about how smooth someone's operation is, while explaining in detail how it works. Three days later some slickster is in jail because of their big mouth.

One thing about it, sitting in jail for even six hours makes you realize just how much of a privilege it is to come and go as you please, along with eating whenever you feel like it. When little things like that are taken away, it makes you appreciate freedom.

Another thing about jail is you lose track of time. They woke us up the next morning for breakfast, and I hadn't the slightest clue as to the time. Marching to the cafeteria single file, we didn't even get to freshen up, although no toiletries were supplied anyway. All you could do was get in line and march.

The cafeteria resembled something you'd see in middle

school, only smaller. We entered the door, turned left, and were handed plastic spoons. A roll-up aluminum gate was raised a foot high, allowing only a view of latex-gloved hands sliding plates underneath.

Laughter and joking among the staff was clearly audible, which served only to remind you of freedom. The meal consisted of watery eggs, half-cooked sausages, toast, milk, and a slice of fruit. Those unfamiliar didn't eat, but to many, the food was just as tasty as what you'd get at a five-star restaurant. As soon as I sat, this big ugly fool reached across the table, helping himself to my milk.

"You don't want this," he said.

"Yes I do."

The next sound heard was my plate slamming upside his head. He raised his fist to swing, but I was too fast, flinging the tray like a boomerang, watching as it connected squarely on his forehead. Before we could rumble, the officers broke it up, hauling us off to individual cells. That meant I'd miss another meal because of someone else.

Thirty minutes later my cell door opened and I was free to go. I passed Jughead and avoided his arm, which grabbed at me. Jumping back, I shot a gob of spit directly in his face. Laughing while the guards shoved me, I heard his useless threats of retaliation.

I was taken to a window and my property returned in a plastic zip-lock baggie displaying my name. Then I was escorted out the door. Once it slammed, I saw Cassandra sitting on a bench nodding. Happy to be free, I knew nonetheless that I hadn't heard the last of Johnson or Hernandez.

"Damn, if that ain't the prettiest face I've seen all day."

"Ooh baby, you're out!"

"Yeah, I'm out cause I didn't do anything."

Leaping to her feet, she hugged me tightly then said, "You, Mr. Jordan, need a bath."

"Your place or mine?" I joked.

"You're so funny," she said, showing all thirty-two.

Arm in arm, we walked out that hellhole and went to her car. She drove to my house, and as I bathed, she cooked. I put on a pair of jeans and t-shirt then sat down to a real sausage-and-egg breakfast.

Cassandra wanted all details of my brief incarceration, so I gave her a scene-by-scene description. By the time I was done, she vowed to never go to jail. I could only smile, because I'd successfully scared her straight.

We finished our meals, then while she washed dishes I fed Iceberg. After that, she drove me to her place to pick up Bertha. She'd taken my car to her crib after leaving Momma's and parked it in her garage. I knew this was the woman for me because when I was down, she was beside me solid as a rock. Walking up to her door, we both noticed her neighbor's drapes close abruptly.

"Hold on baby, I've had enough of this shit," she said while trying to knock a hole through her neighbor's door.

"Cassandra, why you bammin on my door like that?" Nadine asked.

"Look, bitch, I don't appreciate yo ass spyin on me! I

know you been tellin Buckey my business, but I'm gonna put it like this: you stick yo nose in my affairs one more time and I'll stick my foot in yo stanky ass!"

"Wait a minute, who you callin a bitch?"

"I'm calling you a bitch, bitch!"

"Look hoe, ah thank you better get yo ass away from my doe!"

"Nadine, you better stay out my business or it's gonna be you and me."

"Girl, I ain't in yo business, but if you call me out my name again, I'ma come outside an whup yo ass — you know I don't play."

"Nadine, you know what, fuck you!"

"Bitch, fuck you!"

"Fuck wit me if you think you can."

"Bitch, I'ma kick yo ass you don't get away from my doe. What you better do is take yo friend and go home."

"I ain't better do shit except put yo stanky ass in check."

Cassandra began kicking her security gate, challenging Nadine to come outside, but all Nadine did was respond threateningly through her screen.

"I'm calling the police!"

"Call the police, bitch, we gonna settle this shit once and for all."

Grabbing Cassandra by the arm, I led her to her own door, unlocked it, then coaxed her in. All the while she spewed obscenities at Nadine, who seemed to get bolder with her words the further away we got.

Nadine was a pitiful-looking woman with a funny

build. She had small legs with wide hips and behind — the results of sitting on her butt all day watching soaps. She had a pouch in the middle and tiny breasts, but her mug is what caught my attention.

Her lips were torn up, eyes bloodshot, gold hair stood all over her head, and she had rashy ears that were broken out from her cheap costume jewelry.

"That bitch betta not come out — if she does I'll kick her ass!"

Cassandra was so animated that I found it amusing. She came out of the bedroom dressed for battle, wearing jeans, tennis shoes, and a tight-fitting leotard top. Talking to herself about Nadine, she wrapped her braids with a rubber band, removed her jewelry, then applied baby oil to every exposed section of skin.

Witnessing this unexpected fury from her aroused me tremendously. I pulled her into my arms and gave her a kiss full of the lust my body felt. The longer we kissed, the more the fight left her body to be replaced by passion.

Leading me to the bedroom, she began a sensuous assault on my torso while her hands massaged my meat. My penis swelled full of blood and had the look of a miniature baseball bat.

Her lips covered my pole, working it over. The girl brought out feelings in me that had been asleep for a long time. Stripping out of her fighting outfit, she mounted. Working her way down slowly, she rode me the way a jockey rides a racehorse.

Each time I would thrust upward, she would match my intensity with a downward thrust of her own. She bucked and squirmed viciously when all of a sudden her body exploded with a powerful orgasm, triggering mine.

She slumped over my body, resting her head on my chest. The night spent in jail, lack of proper rest, and wonderful lovemaking had me asleep in minutes.

11
strange
bedmates

Buckey rose early Friday at the crack of dawn. Counting his scrill and remaining dope, he realized that he'd need to cop more product before the Fourth. His bank had increased to sixty-five G's and he had three more in rocks, but a larger problem loomed.

Since he'd never sold dope, he had no connections. Before he ran out he would have to remedy the situation. Earl knew many people in the drug trade, and Buckey would make certain his boy hooked him up.

Taking a rare shower, Buckey put on one of his new sweatsuits, hopped in his Caddy, and drove the ten-minute ride to Earl's crib.

Earl was born and raised on the west side but had moved east six months earlier. His neighborhood was dubbed "Funktown" and spanned the area of 5th Avenue to 23rd, bordered by Foothill to East 32nd.

The entire radius was populated by blacks, Latinos, and

Asians, with a few whites sprinkled in for good measure. It was, like many parts of town, a very violent turf.

Although Buckey was known and feared in the west side, the east side was an entirely different matter. There were a lot of Buckeys on that side of the city casting just as deadly a shadow as he did on his turf.

Earl's place was a rundown apartment complex on the corner of 22nd and East 21st. Beige with brown trim, the complex was in serious need of a paint job. Graffiti displaying a balled-up fist with the index and pinky fingers sticking out were visible on every block, Funktown's unofficial logo.

Buckey didn't like venturing too far from home, so he was glad that it was still early with most residents in bed. Over the years he'd had a couple of riffs with some eastside boys, so he knew he had enemies on this side of town.

Seeing Earl's Blazer parked in the driveway, Buckey pulled over and stepped out. He reached for the doorbell, but before he could push it Earl had the door open with that familiar grin on his face.

"Buckey, what brings you out this time of morning? Come in."

"Man, ah need you ta hook me up wit a connection."

"Did Violet tell you me and Slack came over yesterday?"

"Naw, she still asleep, somethin you don't do." They both laughed.

"You hear about Spodie?" Earl asked.

"Naw, what about him?" Buckey lied.

"They found him dead yesterday. Dude who did it is Stoney's brother."

"Stoney's brother?" Buckey's surprise was genuine.

"Yeah, his brother Rainbow, fool who be tryin ta sang."

"You thank he know bout us?"

"It's hard ta say Buck — you know Spodie always run off at the mouth, and niggers will sell they own momma if the price is right."

"Tell me what you know bout dis heah Rainbow."

"Not much, man, but I do know he sposed ta be tough. Drive a money-green Accord, live somewhere out here in the east, work for the city, and I heard he was at Bogie's the other night with yo sister-in-law, sangin to her and shit. My homeys told me they was all lovey-dovey."

"Yeah, ah heard he sposed ta be messin wif Sandra."

"Well, all I can say, Gee, is watch ya back."

"Know das right." They slapped five.

"You need a piece?"

"Naw, dude, ah got Roscoe wit me."

"I heard that — what kinda package you lookin for?"

"What ah need is three thousand dollahs' worth."

"Check it, I know exactly who can handle that."

"Who?"

"My boy Alphonse. Tonio be havin the shit, A-1."

"Where he at?"

"He moves around a lot ta keep five-o off his back, but I got his beeper number."

"Hook me up wit 'im."

"Awight, lemme call 'im."

Earl picked up the phone while Buckey peeped out his pad. To look so bad outside, Earl's place was expensively furnished. He had a solid oak dinette set, brown leather sofa and loveseat, fifty-two-inch color television, marble coffee and end tables, full-size leopard figurines, component set with all the toys, plants, fish tank with assorted colorful fish swimming around, bird cage housing a yellow and black canary, brand new computer, and two Persian rugs.

Buckey knew most of the items were stolen but was impressed nonetheless. He thought it must be nice to live in luxury. Earl's home was a mansion compared to his, and Buckey felt a slight twinge of jealousy. There was no doubt in his mind that he'd get Earl to help furnish his home.

The phone rang and Earl picked up. It was Alphonse responding to the page. Earl went in the kitchen, talking in hushed tones. Buckey could hardly hear him.

The moment Buckey began to get restless, Earl's main squeeze wandered out of the bedroom. She wore a silk negligee that left nothing to the imagination. A large woman, her legs were thick as tree trunks and looked delicious. They were muscular, dark brown, and had not an ounce of flab.

Gigantic nipples stretched her fabric to its limit, and her areolas were clearly visible. She had a small waist and large booty, which switched from side to side with each step she took.

She had a full beautiful face with large lips and pearl-white teeth. She was a full-figured woman in every sense of the word. Buckey could have sworn he saw her pubic hairs sticking out and felt his manhood rise rapidly. Earl finished his conversation, rejoining Buckey on the sofa.

"Buckey, this is my honey Brenda. Brenda, meet Buckey."

"Hello Buckey, it's very nice to meet you," Brenda said.

"Nice ta meet you too. Earl didn't tell me bout you, but now ah know why he be at home so much," Buckey joked.

"Baby, you guys want some coffee?" she asked Earl.

"Yes, dear, that'll be nice."

Brenda headed for the kitchen with Buckey's eyes greedily following her every step of the way. She loved the attention so she put an extra wiggle in her walk. She also knew her man was screwing women all over town.

She hoped Earl would notice the way his friend was drooling at the mouth and become jealous, but Earl just sat there with a silly grin on his face. Once she was out of earshot, they resumed their rap.

"Goddamn Earl, you sho did pick a winner dare."

"See Buck, y'all think they be fat but I know once those clothes come off, it's thick."

"Ah heard dat. I'ma hafta get me one uh dem."

"And do what? Get her and you shot? You know Violet don't play, and judging from the way you was sprawled out yesterday, I don't think you got the energy for nobody but Violet." They both laughed.

"Yeah, Violet be drainin mah ass. Wuz up wif da phone call?"

"My boy Alphonse said he'll hook you up with a quarter-pound for twenty-eight hundred."

"He cain't come down none?"

"Nope, he sells his ounces for seven, but after he gets

to know you and sees that you're a regular client, he'll start hookin you up proper."

"Awight, dat'll work."

"So when you wanna connect?"

Before Buckey could respond, Brenda came from the kitchen with their coffee. Earl excused himself to go to the bathroom.

"Would you like cream and sugar?" she asked Buckey.

"Yeah, heavy on da cream," he said flirtatiously.

Brenda leaned over to pick up his mug, giving him a nice view of her ample bosom. The fact that she didn't cover up left him to think she would play. He knew if his friends came over, Violet would not reveal her assets like that.

Brenda liked the build on Buckey but thought his appearance could use some work. Since she knew Earl was secretly screwing her friend Shantay daily while she was at work, this might be her best revenge — to fuck his friend. Earl returned from the bathroom then told Buckey he was going to take a shower and get dressed.

"Make yourself at home, dude, I'll be ready in ten minutes."

"Awight Earl, I'mo drank dis coffee an watch yo big screen."

"Brenda, I'll be in the shower, baby," he yelled.

"Okay, honey," she answered from the kitchen.

Once Earl started the shower Brenda called out, "Buckey, can you come get the cream for me? I can't reach it."

Buckey went to the kitchen and froze in his tracks.

Brenda was reaching for the cream on the top shelf with her negligee climbing halfway up her butt. Buckey felt his hardness rise to full attention. Being as bold as he was, he jerked down his sweatpants and stated: "Ah thank you wont dis."

Brenda turned around to look and got soaking wet with what she saw. Buckey had a giant pole, longer *and* fatter than Earl's. It looked like a lethal weapon. Her eyes became big as saucers and her mind went blank. She stood gazing at his meat, imagining how good it would feel inside her vagina.

Walking to him in a trance, she dropped to her knees and began sucking it like a popsicle. Buckey felt his beef throbbing from her attention, because not only was she hungrily taking it in, she swallowed twice as much as Violet could.

Lifting her to her feet, he bent her over the sink and penetrated from behind, filling her like never before. He pumped violently and she loved every bit of it. They heard the water shut off in the bathroom, which caused him to begin a furious assault on her cunt.

Brenda was opening and closing her fingers, biting her lip, shaking her head from side to side, doing everything she could to stop from screaming. She knew this would not be the last time he hit it because no dick had ever felt this good.

Buckey exploded inside her then pulled up his sweatpants, telling her to let Earl know he'd call him later.

"Meet me at the Coliseum Motel in half an hour," she said then kissed him savagely.

"Okay," he agreed.

She sprayed air freshener to cover their scent, stuffed her hole with a paper towel, and headed for the bedroom to get dressed. Buckey poured his coffee down the drain, walked out the door, and drove off. Earl exited the bathroom to find Brenda fully dressed and Buckey gone.

"Babe, Buckey split?"

"Yes, he said he'd call you later."

"You on your way to work?"

"Yes dear, I have a lot to do today," she said, dreaming of Buckey.

"Well, have fun. I have to fix Shantay's dripping faucet — you don't mind, do you?"

"Not at all. Have a nice day, baby."

Brenda knew the only drip Earl would clog would be on Shantay's body but she didn't care today. While he was sticking his skinny pole in Shantay, she'd enjoy a full-course meal. Cutting out, she drove in the opposite direction of her job. One minute later, Earl was on the phone with Shantay.

Buckey stopped at a liquor store to purchase a fifth of brandy along with a two-liter Coke. Next he drove to the taco truck on High Street and ordered two steak burritos with sour cream and cheese. There were many taco trucks situated around the city, but to Buckey the one on High Street provided the best Mexican food. They would also give you red or green sauce, radishes, green onions, and jalapeno peppers wrapped in foil with your meal.

The Coliseum Motel sat right off I-880 at the High Street exit. Down the block was a drive-in movie theater that doubled as a flea market during the day. Across from that was the city's automotive maintenance yard.

Factories and assorted businesses saturated the rest of the area. The parking lot was in the center of the motel, so your car was hidden from the passing traffic. Buckey pulled into the lot smiling as Brenda was about to enter their room. Getting out, he jogged up behind her.

"I thought you would be waiting," she said teasingly.

"Ah would'a bin, but ah stopped ta get us some grub," he said, handing her the food.

"Ooh, the truck?" she inquired.

"Nuttin but," he answered, proud of his selection.

Brenda called her job claiming illness, then started fixing their plates while Buckey went outside to the ice machine. Returning to the room, he poured them both a stiff mixture of brandy and Coke on the rocks. She was already naked, and the sight of her huge breasts made him hard immediately. He undressed and they ate in the nude.

"So how long you been knowin Earl?"

"Ah been knowin him all mah life."

"Then you know he be fuckin all over town?"

"Baby, ah ain't one ta tell on another brutha."

"Well, I'll put it like this, I know he be giving away dick like the Salvation Army give away clothes. All I wanted to do was get even, but after having you, his ass is out."

Buckey smiled, content with the fact that his homey's woman chose him after sampling his meat one time. Brenda finished her food while Buckey still had half a burrito remaining. Gulping down her drink then pouring another, she buried her face in his groin, devouring his dick as he ate the burrito.

Tossing the last of the food on the floor, he threw her on her back and plunged deep inside her steaming hole. She'd never been so full and moaned loudly, which spurred him on to screw her harder. Juice poured down the crack of her butt, and although she was wetter than she'd ever been, she was still full to capacity.

She released multiple orgasms while he pumped away as if they'd just started. As she professed her love for him, Buckey put his mouth to the pillow and laughed. He knew now that he could have her whenever he chose, and if he asked her to leave Earl she probably would.

Buckey was surprised by Brenda's flexibility due to the fact that he'd always believed the myth that full-figured women had no stamina. Now he knew that wasn't so because her legs were spread just as wide and lifted as high as every other woman he'd known.

Once he finally came, she slid down his torso and resumed sucking. This action made his hardness return, so he put it back inside her body. By the time she finally dozed off it was almost noon.

He went in the bathroom and did a sorry job of washing the smell off his body. Getting dressed and taking the bottle of brandy, he bounced.

Buckey hadn't enjoyed a piece like that in ages. Sex with Violet was good, but they were both familiar with one another's body. Brenda was new and refreshing, and the fact that she moaned and screamed constantly only made it better.

Parking in the driveway, he hoped Violet would still be asleep. A note on the table informed him that she had gone across town to the supermarket with friends. He was relieved because since they spent every day together, he never had time to cheat.

Besides, if she were home he knew she'd want sex as soon as he hit the door, and right now he was too tired for that. Pouring himself a drink in a dirty glass, he downed it then plopped on the sofa and fell asleep.

12
DEAD-END CLUE

Johnson and Hernandez reported for their usual shift and were relieved to find that Spitz had taken a vacation day. They were glad he was starting his holiday weekend early. This meant they could get plenty of work done.

Spitz would always get in the way, the classic example of an incompetent boss. Most of the detectives hoped Johnson would be the next Deputy Chief because he was fair, analytical, had common sense, and had worked his way up through the ranks.

"What we got today, Manny?"

"Nate, we got a robbery suspect who wants to work a deal, says he knows who did the Jordan shooting and will give us a name if we give him a break."

"Where is he?"

"He's in the interrogation room."

"Let's go."

They walked down the hallway to criminal investigations to question the suspect with possible information on their case. The prisoner's name was Eddie Turner, a small-time hood with an extensive record.

He had been in and out of criminal institutions since the age of twelve and had grown up on the west side, so he probably had pertinent information.

"Alright Turner, what you got?" Johnson asked, getting to the point.

"I got what you want, but what's in it for me?" Turner retorted.

"What do you want?"

"I want this bullshit charge dropped. I didn't do shit and y'all know it — I was just around and since I got a record, they brought me in. I should sue OPD for this shit."

"Look, Turner, they got you red-handed; now if you got information on a murder, we will tell the judge that you assisted in solving the case. I don't have the authority to guarantee you anything."

"Well, I want to talk to whoever can guarantee me something."

"Look punk, you're a six-time loser facing the three-strike law — you ain't in the position to bargain. Tell me what you know and you have my word that we'll ask the judge for leniency."

"Man, what you take me for, a fool?"

"Let's go, Manny, this trick ain't got nothing." They rose to leave.

"Wait, man, the dude who did the shootin's name is

Slack — he stay in Chestnut Court, I don't know his real name."

"How do you know it was him?" Johnson inquired.

"I know the dude, man, he be shootin people all the time, he just never get caught."

Johnson and Hernandez knew Slack well, having hauled him in many times for questioning about murders. In each case they were forced to release him due to insufficient evidence, no murder weapon, and his consistently airtight alibis.

His specialty was killing. They knew it and Turner did too, so they knew he wouldn't testify in a court of law. That would be murder in itself because Slack would surely kill Turner if he even knew they were talking now.

"Okay, Turner, we'll see what we can do," Johnson stated.

"Do it quick, man," Turner said as they walked out.

"Manny, pull up the file on Slack."

"Consider it done."

Slack's real name was Robert Henderson, and his file was thick as a dictionary. OPD was mystified as to how someone could have a jacket like that but never be charged with anything. Johnson and Hernandez knew they had nothing now, but hoped like always Slack would make a mistake, as all criminals do sooner or later.

Manny returned with the files, which he and Nate poured over, reacquainting themselves with Slack.

"Manny, let's go pick up the bum."

"What can we charge him with, Nate?"

"Suspicion."

"It won't stick."

"I know, I just want to let him know we're around."

"Okay partner, let's go."

They got in their unmarked car and headed for Slack's house. He lived in the Chestnut Court housing complex, which was located on Grand Avenue. Two blocks from McClymond's High, Chestnut Court was a rundown Section 8 project better known for its excellent city-run Head Start program than anything else.

There were many law-abiding citizens living there and welfare mothers doing all they could to make a better life, but once darkness fell, the riff-raff ruled the compound. It's the same old story in most projects. When it gets dark, if you ain't cool, stay in the house. You were essentially a prisoner in your own home.

The detectives hooked a left on Market, drove two blocks, then made a right. As they pulled over to park, Slack rode right past them headed to Buckey's. They didn't see him and he didn't see them, all too preoccupied in thought to notice anyone or anything.

Slack drove like always, fast and with an open bottle of T-bird sitting in his lap. He had given the majority of his share of Stoney's money to his woman Yolanda. They'd grown up together, known each other since childhood, and had four offspring.

Although Slack never held an honest job in his life, he was a decent provider for his family, due in large part to his criminal activities.

Yolanda Henderson was a mean woman. She'd get full of happy juice then profanity would spill out her mouth.

Violence was something she enjoyed, often jumping on other women along with fist-fighting Slack like a man.

When he came home with money they had good times, but when he came home broke, they fought. She was from a family of nine, all poor, rowdy, and fourth-generation welfare. If you got into a rumble with one of the Minors, which was her maiden name, you knew more of those fools would be coming later.

She was a big six two, weighing two hundred pounds with large hands that made even larger fists. Her daily attire was usually stretch pants with oversized t-shirts and tennis shoes. Her hair had fallen out from letting her sisters put hot combs to it daily while growing up, so she wore head scarves.

A long scar ran from beneath her temple to her chin, the result of a vicious rumble she'd had as a teenager with a girl she thought wanted Slack. Overpowering the girl, she took the knife and stabbed her to death, but didn't do any time because the police ruled it self-defense.

Yolanda received Section 8 for nearly twenty years and considered herself in better financial shape than most working people. She'd often brag, "I pay a hundred and twenty dollars for rent, get nine hundred a month in cash, three fifty in food stamps, and medical free. When my kids get eighteen I'll play crazy then get disability checks the rest of my life."

She didn't realize that the crazy checks would be small, food stamp allotment reduced, or she would have no retirement nest egg to enjoy in her later years. She lived for here and now. Most fourth-generation welfare recipients thought the same as Yolanda.

The drug dealers and local hoods saw Johnson and Hernandez pull over, then scattered like rats fleeing a tomcat. Manny noticed everyone disappear and shook his head in disgust.

"Nate, I don't know about your people. If they're not doing anything wrong, why are they so quick to disappear?"

"Manny, these people are not a clear representation of the entire black community. There are many hardworking, law-abiding citizens in this neighborhood who are just as disgusted as you about the lack of morals or decency these idiots display."

"Well, if there are I never see them."

"You have the mindset of a cowboy or rogue cop who feels as if the flatlands are a jungle."

"Partner, I know you don't like it, but the truth is the truth."

"Manny, look, let's go get Henderson and save this debate for another day, okay?"

"Okay Nate, whatever you say."

One day Johnson knew he would check Manny, but like always, now was not the time. They crossed the street and went into the complex, which covered an entire city block and had a driveway leading to a parking lot in the center.

The childcare building was next to the lot, with the garbage dumpsters off to the side of that. A children's play area was to the right, and there were several walk-in entrance/exits.

Painted beige with brown trim, the structures' color scheme changed every ten years. Three stories high all the way around, it had the appearance of a fortress. Poverty was a way of life on the west side, and this complex was a prime example. Broken glass and litter were everywhere, sheets hung on windows instead of curtains or blinds, and filthy kids ran around with snotty noses.

The detectives walked up to Yolanda's door and knocked. She recognized them immediately because they were the arresting officers for the stabbing beef. They'd also harass her man about every unsolved murder on the west side.

"Well, if it ain't Fric n Frac — what did we do now?" Yolanda demanded sarcastically.

"Mrs. Henderson, is your husband home?" Hernandez asked.

"Naw, he gone."

"Where did he go?"

"Ta hell and back for all I know. Look, if y'all don't have a warrant then get the fuck away from mah damn doe, I ain't got shit foe ya."

"When he returns, ask him to call us," Johnson said while sliding his card through the door.

"Why is it every time y'all got an unsolved case, you come here?"

"Just ask him to get in touch with me," Johnson said as they walked off.

Manny walked back to the car in a rage. If he ever got the chance he vowed to beat the shit out of that ugly broad. Johnson didn't necessarily like Yolanda, but he understood that she considered police the enemy.

He also knew that the way she talked was how she had expressed herself all her life. "She doesn't know any better" is how he explained the vulgarity and sarcasm to

Manny. Satisfied that the point had been made, they drove back to the station.

Slack returned home a half hour later and immediately began getting his arsenal together. Yolanda told him about the visit from "Fric 'n Frac" but Slack didn't seem to care. His mind was on the job at hand. He wondered if they wanted to question him about Stoney's death. He had killed so many people in his life and been hauled down to the station so many times that he really didn't care what they wanted. Plopping down in a chair at the kitchen table, he waited as she fixed his plate.

Yolanda was a very good cook, with the skill to take scraps and make nice meals out of them. Today she had neck bones, black-eyed peas, and candied yams along with hot-water corn bread. When she cooked peas, beans, greens, or cabbage she always added salt pork, ham shanks or hocks, fried meat grease, and lots of seasonings.

Her kitchen was filled with cast-iron skillets of various sizes, plus all types of pots, knives, and cooking utensils. The walls were decorated with pot holders, extra-large spoons, forks, and scripture plates. Under the wall phone hung a calendar filled with telephone numbers. Above that was a clock painted brass which resembled a skillet. Yolanda's kitchen was her sanctuary.

The remainder of the apartment was shabby. Their sofa and loveseat were covered with sheets to hide all the rips and tears. An outdated stereo with several different brand components stacked on top was a fashion disaster. The rest of the furnishings were very old, but to Yolanda's credit, her home was clean.

While Slack ate, he lubricated his guns with Three-in-

One cleaner. Meticulous, he always made sure his weapons were in top working order. Today he would use a high-powered rifle with a scope and a 357 Magnum.

Yolanda sat admiring her man. She knew when he went on jobs he didn't feel like talking. His mind was deep in thought, developing a plan. Slack finished his meal and told Yolanda to wake him at five-thirty sharp. Lying on the sofa, he took a nap.

13
TiGHT BaCKUP

Violet returned home at three with a car-load of groceries. She had given her friend Sophia a hundred dollars in stamps, full tank of gas, and more food than her icebox would hold. One thing Violet never did was shop alone. But she hated when Buckey tagged along because he was restless, impatient, and complained constantly. Waking him up, she yakked excitedly.

"Baby, me and Sophia been everywhere. I loaded up for the Fourth and told all our friends to come over. Look at this — I got a case of ribs, hot links, hamburgers, weanies, steaks, roast beef, a ham, lunch meat, and chicken wangs. Plus, I got poke chops, neckbones, ham hocks, ox tails, turkey wangs — baby, I got everythang they had."

"Where you get dat from?" he asked, not really caring.

"Sophia took me to a meat market she know bout, one of those Arab stowes on the east side. I got catfish, red snapper, and perch. Ooh baby, then we went to the bread stowe and loaded up on light bread, buns, cupcakes, pies, cinnamon rolls, I got everything!"

Violet always got excited when she grocery shopped because it was something she didn't do often. Before she was done she would show Buckey each item with an individual explanation of why she bought it.

"Baby, we went to Canned Foods and I loaded up the cabinets. We got enough food for at least three months. I got...."

"Who sposed ta be comin heah on da Fourth?" Buckey interrupted.

"Anybody who wants to. I invited yo momma, sister, and told them ta tell all yo cousins. My family comin, plus Sophia and Gerald, Tanisha and Mark, and you can tell yo friends. We got enough food for all of 'em, then some."

Violet was proud of her accomplishment and wanted everyone to know that she and Buckey were living large. Buckey dreaded it already — he was not an entertainer and didn't look forward to having a house full of people at his place.

One thing he did know was that when his woman set her mind to something, it was as good as done, so he really had no choice. Rising up, he poured himself a shot and watched Violet finish her QVC presentation on each item. Once she paused to catch her breath, he spoke.

"Ah got a connection on some moe dope."

"Oh, you do? Who is it?"

"I'ont know, some dude Earl know. We sposed ta make a pickup tanite."

"Sounds good to me."

"Ah'm bout ta go ta Wino Park and sell some moe — you wanna come?"

"Naw, baby, you go ahead. Sophia's comin over ta help me clean up the house. I need to get it straight for Sunday."

Buckey gave Violet a kiss and walked out with what felt like the beginning of a headache. Sometimes her nonstop chatter did that to him. Starting up his engine, he shifted to drive and pulled off. Glancing in his rear-view mirror, he spotted Slack turning the corner in his beat-up Toyota. Buckey pulled over and got out.

"Slack, baby, wuz up?"

"Oh, you finally woke up, huh?" They laughed and shook hands.

"Man, ah was tired yesterday."

"Yeah, tell me anythang, Miss Violet musta been layin it on yo ass again." They both laughed some more.

"Naw, dat ain't it, you know who controls dat shit, ah was just tired."

"Dude, you hear bout Spodie?" Slack asked while taking a swig of T-bird.

"Yeah, Earl tole me dis moanin."

"I went by the house — his mom say the funeral gone be Wednesday."

"Earl say Stoney's brutha did it," Buckey stated unconvincingly.

"Yea, they arrested Rainbow but let him out this morning."

"Why dey do dat?"

"Didn't have nothing to hold him on. One of my boys, Eddie Turner, got picked up last night for robbery and told his sister, who told me."

"Ah was tellin Earl dat we probly gone hafta deal wif dis heah Rainbow foe all is said and done."

"Check it — what's on yo agenda for today?"

"Ah was on mah way ta sell some moe dope. Tanite ah'm sposed ta cop from one uh Earl's hookups. Dude's name is Tonio or some shit like dat."

"Alphonse, I've heard of him, he's a heavyweight. I think you need me for backup."

"Ah no das right, shidd."

"What time is the transaction gonna take place?"

"At seven — ah gotta call Earl at six ta find out where."

"Do it like this, man — meet me at Earl's pad at six then we'll go from there. What you need to do is find out where the deal gonna go down before I get there, because I already know he'll say the only ones who can come is you and him."

"Dat'll work, ah be dare."

"Cool."

Slack got in his hooptie and sped off. Buckey knew he was going to get his artillery together. One thing he admired about Slack was the fact that Slack considered any deal could result in a double-cross, so he planned his strategy accordingly.

With Slack, if something did go wrong he was always

ready for it. Buckey drove to the park and immediately began making sales. The scene was identical to the day before, with dope fiends and alcoholics everywhere. Homeless people slept on benches, anything possible occurring in the restrooms, along with dice and domino games going continuously.

By five o'clock Buckey had made six hundred, so he went home to stash his dope and get his money and pistol. After telling Violet his plans, he drove to Earl's. Pulling up, he noticed Earl's Blazer missing, but Brenda's Legend was there. Seeing this, he smiled. She came to the door wearing a loose-fitting summer dress, and when she opened it the reflection caused by the sun revealed her entire shape. Brenda closed and locked the door behind him then planted a passionate kiss on his lips.

"Earl just left, said he had to put another washer on Shantay's sink. He thinks you were going to call at six. I'm glad you came instead — all I could think about today was you."

As the words flowed from Brenda's mouth she kissed his neck, chest, and shoulders. She was sprung and he knew it, proud of himself for springing her in one day.

"Earl could never satisfy me the way you do. I don't even want him anymore. If you want me as your woman, you got me. Let me fix you something to eat."

She bounced into the kitchen and fixed him a giant plate of leftover lasagna while singing to herself. Buckey relaxed on the sofa, contemplating his options. She had a good job with Internal Revenue, a thick body, would worship him til the day she died, and gave wonderful sex.

Violet was great in bed also, down for him one hundred and fifty percent, thought just like he did, and was dangerous. This girl seemed timid so for now he would stay with Violet and talk Brenda into kicking Earl to the curb. That way he could have his cake and eat it too.

"Yo, baby!" Buckey hollered.

"Yes, dear?"

"Did Earl tell you where dis meetin sposed ta take place?"

"Yes, baby, he told me you guys are supposed to meet at Eastmont in the bottom parking lot by the restaurants."

"Yo, write dat down fa me on a lil piece uh paper."

"Okay."

Brenda handed him the information along with a kiss and his plate. He wolfed the food down hungrily then went to the fridge and poured a large glass of Kool-Aid. She watched starry-eyed as he gulped it down.

She did not care that his cornrows needed re-braiding, body stank, and language left a lot to be desired. Her mind was focused on the way he made her body feel. Brenda's parents had always told her to avoid guys like Buckey who were dangerous, deadly, and possessed no morals.

Right now she could care less, because her bell had been rung like never before so she was stuck on stupid. Earl walked in with Slack right behind him, already engaged in a heated discussion.

"Slack, you can't come, man — they don't even know Buckey, let alone you," Earl stated forcefully.

"Dude, I need to be there to watch y'all backs."

"Man, if you come that's gonna blow the whole deal. Buckey, tell Slack he can't go," Earl demanded.

"Slack, dude's right, man. Look, ah meet you at mah crib roun bout nine. Come on, ah walk you out ta yo car."

Slack gave Earl a deadly stare and walked out without even saying goodbye. Once outside, Buckey slipped him the note written by Brenda and told him, "Be dare an when you see da whites uh dey eyes . . ."

"Shoot 'em up bang bang" Slack stated, smiling as he drove off.

Buckey returned to the house, instantly amused by the conversation coming out of Earl's bedroom.

"BITCH, I came to your job to take you to lunch and they said YOU CALLED IN SICK! Where were you?" Earl screamed.

"I told you since I wasn't feeling well, I went to the doctor to be checked. Since I didn't have an appointment I HAD TO WAIT!" she shouted, "and I'm not your bitch!"

"Where were you the rest of the day?" he demanded.

"I was home, where were YOU?"

"Aw, fuck you."

"You wish you could."

Earl slammed the bedroom door and joined Buckey on the sofa. He knew he'd done wrong with Shantay but wondered about Brenda. Something wasn't right, he just didn't know what. Maybe it was time to leave her fat ass and take Shantay up on her offer.

In a million years he never would have guessed that Brenda was screwing Buckey. He thought Violet was the only woman crazy enough to be with his nasty, ill-mannered friend.

"Man, she fuckin somebody else," Earl said.

"How you know dat?" Buckey inquired.

"Cause the bitch didn't go to work but tried to play it off like she did."

"Maybe she was sick, Earl."

"Dude, that hoe was not sick — I ain't no fool."

"Dig it, let's go get da dope."

"Alright, let's raise the fuck up outta here."

They walked out, with Earl slamming the door. Buckey hopped in the passenger side of Earl's blue with white trim four-by-four. Fully loaded, the truck had been purchased from a dude Earl knew who specialized in stolen vehicles.

He and his crew would steal a car or truck, then change the identification number. Paying off DMV employees, they were provided phony registration papers, stickers, pink slips, and license plates.

The total cost was usually less than four thousand dollars, so the buyer would get a fairly new ride for less than one year's worth of car notes. You would have to buy a new ignition switch and get keys made for the trunk and doors if you didn't want the vehicle stolen from you.

Earl popped in a BOYZ II MEN tape and sped off peeling rubber. Still upset about Brenda, he took Foothill riding in silence. Buckey rode in silence also, with his mind preoccupied by the transaction about to occur.

With no major retail stores, Eastmont resembled an indoor flea market more than a mall. All of the national chains had moved out, leaving only nickel-and-dime independent vendors along with Asians selling cheap gold that was more plated than solid. The mall closed on Fridays at six, so the place was deserted.

Hitting a rounding curve on 73rd, Earl drove two blocks down and turned right into the mall. After another sharp right, he headed for the lower-level back parking lot, which due to lack of activity had been roped off and closed for years.

One section of rope was broken, allowing people to use this area for drug deals, a lovers' rendezvous, or as a place to get high. Poorly lit, the place was saturated with broken glass and overturned trash cans.

Five minutes later Alphonse arrived. He drove a black Bronco monster truck. High yellow and handsome, Alphonse was what Buckey called a "Pretty Boy." He had long black hair braided in a ponytail and was draped in gold. Buckey took an immediate dislike to him.

Stepping out on the passenger side was Big T. Six foot six, midnight black, and ugly, Big T was a very violent individual. He wore blue Levis, cowboy boots, blue-and-white striped button-down shirt, black mid-thigh leather coat, and a godfather brim.

His hands were extremely large and his demeanor nasty. The Colt 45 displayed in his waistband only increased the aura surrounding this man. Buckey considered him dangerous.

Scanning the area, Buckey saw a solitary figure crouched on an unused car ramp one hundred yards away. Slack was taking dead aim through his scope. Buckey felt better knowing he held the element of surprise.

Only five feet ten, weighing one hundred and fifty pounds, Alphonse was accustomed to talking big-time shit. He disrespected everyone because he knew if anybody messed with him, Big T would beat 'em down. It didn't take much for his bodyguard to go off — he made his living off violence and intimidation.

"Earl, what's up, my nigger?"

"Tonio, what's up?" They embraced.

"Ain't shit, man. So this your boy, huh?"

"Yeah, this my boy, Buckey. Buckey meet Tonio."

"What up, dog, glad to do business with you," Tonio greeted.

"Look, let's get down ta bidness," Buckey said with sarcasm.

"We get down to business when I say so, nigger. I don't even know your black ass."

"Aw, fuck you, punk, you ain't gotta sell me nothin — ah'll get mah dope from somebody else."

"That's what you have to do now because I wouldn't sell you shit if you were the last customer on Earth, you no-talking motherfucker."

Alphonse was animated, with his finger pointing and other hand gestures, but he made sure Big T stood between him and Buckey. Big T moved forward in Buckey's direction, while Buckey began backing up.

"Man, said he ain't got no business with you — that means leave," Big T demanded.

"Ah leave when ah get ready, you stupid-ass flunkey."

Big T grabbed Buckey by the collar and drew back his beefy arm, aiming for the nose. Buckey struggled but was no match for the bigger man. The moment Big T started to release his punch, a shot rang out and he fell to the pavement.

The bullet lodged in his right arm, and if he hadn't cocked it so high while punching he would have been dead. Slack always shot for the temple. Big T reached for his gun, and as he pulled it out another slug caught him in the chest. Blood gushed from his body while he kept struggling to get up.

Seizing the moment, Buckey bum-rushed Tonio, attempting to overpower him. Buckey was the bigger and stronger of the two, but Tonio had been a state-meet-caliber wrestler in high school. Realizing that his foe was slowly gaining the advantage, Buckey dug his thumbs into both of Tonio's eye sockets.

Bulldozing Tonio into the monster truck, Buckey rammed his opponent's head savagely on the fender. Tonio maneuvered a duck-under wrestling move, slamming Buckey's face into the side panel. Buckey reached for his piece from his waistband, but before he could get it out Tonio locked him in a bear hug.

The two men began a life-or-death struggle with the gun pointing skyward. Buckey controlled it but Tonio's fingers were vice-locked to his wrists, with neither man holding a clear advantage. Earl stood stark still, frozen in his tracks. It had all blown up so fast he couldn't decide whether to drive off or help Buckey.

Slack continued to fire at Big T, whose pistol was aimed directly at Earl's back. Big T pulled the trigger just as one of Slack's bullets punctured his heart. Big T would not be intimidating anyone else — he lay motionless, dead.

Earl stumbled forward with searing pain scorching his back, then fell down. Alphonse and Buckey tripped over his body, with the gun flying away from Buckey's hand as it hit the ground. Tonio had the better angle, allowing him to reach the weapon first.

Grabbing it off the asphalt he pointed it at Buckey, aimed, and fired. Buckey snatched Earl from the ground, shoving him into Tonio. The force of the blast knocked Earl back two steps. Seeing the gaping hole in his chest caused Earl's body to spasm. Shaking violently with foam pouring from the corners of his mouth, Earl went into shock.

Tonio fired away at Buckey, who'd found refuge behind the four-by-four. Slack got off a bull's-eye hit directly to Tonio's temple. He crumbled to the pavement in a heap, with blood pouring out of his brain. The weapon fell harmlessly to the ground.

Buckey rifled through Tonio's pockets, taking his money, wallet, dope, and jewels. Picking up the gun, he ran in the direction of Slack, who busily wiped all fingerprints off his rifle. He left it there, a useless clue for five-o.

They ran up the ramp to Slack's car, which ironically was parked in front of Eastmont's police substation. The office was only open weekdays from nine to five, a fact that always hit a nerve with east-side residents who'd repeatedly warned police that most of the violence and crime occurred in the evening.

East-side residents wanted a twenty-four/seven station handling all aspects of law enforcement. This place issued taxicab permits, had an abandoned car unit, and housed the lowrider police car along with a souped-up Harley.

Jumping in the hooptie, Buckey gave Slack a well-deserved handshake.

"Thanks, man, ah owe you one."

"Naw, you don't, Buck. It's like I told you, I always got ya back."

They laughed out the lot, heading up 73rd towards the 580 freeway. Buckey counted the loot, which totaled four thousand in cash, twelve in dope, and by his estimate, maybe five in jewels. Breaking off half of everything, Buckey passed it to Slack.

"Dese ropes is fo Yolanda, wit da rest you do what you wont."

"That's right on, Buckey."

"Take me ta Earl's pad fa mah ride."

"Awight boss, you sure you don't want me to get rid of that pistol?"

"Naw, man, ah mo keep Roscoe wif me."

"I hear ya, spote."

Slack sped toward Earl's house while Buckey reclined in the seat, letting his mind dream.

14
commitment

I awoke at six to the sweet aroma of chicken invading my nostrils. Trailing the scent to the kitchen, I walked up behind Cassandra and wrapped my arms around her waist.

She was busily preparing a meal of fried chicken, red beans, rice, gravy, and corn bread. Her method of cooking yardbird was similar to many restaurants. She would wash, season, then bake uncovered, allowing it time to cool when done. Next, the pieces were dipped in buttermilk then flour before deep-frying.

The red beans were washed then placed in boiling water along with a tad of fried meat grease. Seasoning, salt pork, ham shanks, onions, garlic, and peppers were added for flavor.

Using two packets of gravy mix, she followed instructions on the label. Once that was done she added flour, water, onions, teriyaki, and soy sauce. I must admit the smell was exquisite.

Taking a small box of store-bought corn bread along with an egg and milk, Cassandra whipped up a creamy batter. Adding sugar plus the excess butter from the pan gave it the personal touch she seemed to pride herself on.

I took a shower and got dressed before taking a seat at the table, admiring her skills. One thing I loved was a woman who could burn. She fixed our plates, said a prayer, then joined me at the table for what proved to be a very delicious meal.

"Baby, this is off the hook."

"Thanks. I usually don't cook in July because my kids spend this month with my parents."

"Where do your parents live?"

"In San Diego — that's where I'm from," she answered while licking chicken juice off her fingers.

"What do they do down in Southern Cali?"

"Well, when I lived there we would go to Tijuana on weekends."

"And do what?"

"You've never been there?" She seemed surprised.

"Not yet," I said with a smirk on my face.

"Silly, we'd go to Revolution Road and party — the nightclubs are open twenty-four/seven."

"Nightclubs? How many?"

"I don't know, probably twenty. They are all next to

each other, block after block. People come from all over the world, and every club hands out free shots of tequila just to lure you inside."

"Oh, I see, they make a fortune on the price of admission."

"They don't charge to get in because they figure if you get tipsy, you'll stay and spend money."

"So if I want to drink my shot and leave, then go next door and do the same thing, I can?"

"YES."

"Then you gotta take me so I can get drunk for free. What kind of music do they play?"

"Rainbow, you so crazy!" she laughed.

"I'm serious, I don't want to get my head bad then do the salsa, samba, or whatever the hell they do." Cassandra was cracking up. "Each club plays their own style so you can choose from top 40, rap, country, or Spanish. You can hear what they're playing outside."

"It's that loud?"

"Yes, baby, yes."

"What else they got?"

"Let's see, they got taco carts on every corner, clothing stores with cheap prices, jewelers, and Kahlua outlets."

"What you use to make brandy separators?"

"Yeah. They sell blankets, sombreros, lighters, plus all size bottles of Kahlua. The stores are even painted and built as replicas of the drink." She finished her meal then continued, "That seventeen-dollar bottle of Kahlua I saw at your house can be bought for eight in Mexico."

"Girl, you lyin," I said.

"No, I'm not, and if you ever want me to prove it just let me know."

"Okay, BOOK US A PLANE TA-NITE!" I said in my Eddie impersonation.

"Rainbow, you sick!" She was happy to know something I didn't.

"Alright, when it's time to pick up your kids, I'll drive you down there and we'll go to Tijuana."

"Okay, but there's one thing you should know first."

"See, I knew there was a catch somewhere. Anytime something sounds too good to be true, it usually is."

"There's no catch," she laughed.

"What is it then?"

"Nothing, it's just that when you go, you don't drive into Tijuana, you park at the border and walk."

"Why would you do that?"

"BECAUSE baby, if you drive over, you'll be walking back."

"Now why would I walk back if I drove in?"

"Your car will get stolen," she said, serious.

I nearly choked on my food getting up from the table. The more I laughed the funnier her statement became. Cassandra saw how hilarious that was to me, then picked up the laugh bug too.

"Okay, baby," I said, "then we'll rent a car."

"Ca ... ca ... ca ... can't do that!" She was tickled to death.

"Why not?"

"Cau ... cau ... cause the rental agencies stipulate that

you can't take their cars across the bor-bor-bor-BORDER!!"
she shrieked.

I leaned on the wall laughing because that was the funniest conversation I'd had in a long time. At that moment I felt closer to Cassandra than any woman I had ever known. She was just my flavor, and I secretly hoped our relationship would blossom even though we both had failed marriages plus children.

Having no plans for the evening, we decided to walk the lake. Leaving my car in her garage, I drove hers instead. Stopping at the crib to pick up Iceberg, I grabbed my poop scoop, a grocery bag, and paper towels. Anytime I walked my dog, I was always prepared to clean up his mess.

Cassandra followed me to my truck and Iceberg jumped in back. My truck is an old '82 Chevy that I use for hauling and odd jobs. It's also used to help people move furniture, but the main reason I bought it was for Iceberg.

I didn't allow Iceberg in Bertha because he felt it was his privilege to ride in front. He would continually lick my face, slobber on the seats, and block my view with his wagging tail.

Midnight blue with gold interior, the truck was in decent shape to be so old. But it swallowed gas and oil like my boy Luther did liquor. Iceberg stood at attention in back, and I could never determine if he was trying to avoid the wind or letting it slap him in the face. He didn't seem to care because he was just happy to be going somewhere.

Situated in the heart of Oaktown, Lake Merritt is one of the city's crown jewels, a beautiful three-and-one-half-mile circle of jogging track, greenery, and water. Tonight the players were out in full force looking for honeys.

Oaktown is a diverse multi-racial melting pot with the lake its showplace. On one side is Lakeshore Avenue, consisting mainly of apartments with all balconies facing the sparkling water. Tenants can sit on their decks and people-watch, eat, or entertain with a splendid view of downtown, the Bay Bridge, and San Francisco skyline.

The entire area is a high-rent district so you pay for location. In addition to Lake Merritt there is a small grassy-knoll park with restrooms, and one block beyond that, tennis courts and a bakery. To the south sits a convention center, and right behind that, Laney College, whose green neon sign perched atop the administration building can be seen for miles.

Lakeside Drive at the opposite end of the lake is home to the city's main library, recreation department offices, boat docks, and a beautiful lakeside restaurant with a breathtaking view. There's also a park with putting greens where office workers practice their golf games during lunch.

To the north is Grand Avenue, home to specialty stores, mini-markets, and restaurants. Grand meets the lake's main entrance, which houses a garden center that is rented for receptions and parties.

A tiny wooden cottage houses snakes and other reptiles. It sits next to a snack bar, duck pond with feeding area, sailboat house, and in the distance Children's Fairyland.

The summer spot to chill is a patch of grass on a sloped

hill. People bask in the sun, have picnics, or simply watch cars roll through the one-way stretch.

Many of the cleanest rides in the Bay Area converge on the lake each weekend. Paying a two-buck entry fee, they drive through bumper to bumper just to show off their hoopties, while roller skaters whizz by displaying their best moves.

We walked slowly, talking about any- and everything that came to mind, like work problems, family members, goals, dreams, and wishes. I felt comfortable in Cassandra's company because we were on the same page.

She finally cooled on Iceberg too after I explained that dogs are a man's best friend — especially a man without a steady woman to love and share his joy, pain, success, or failure.

I went inside a mini market and purchased a pint of brandy while Cassandra struggled with Iceberg, nearly letting him in the store. The store owner was not amused, but I found the scene hilarious.

Our hand-holding turned into her arm around my waist with my free arm cuddling her shoulder. We walked peacefully around the rest of the lake back to the truck. Once there, we talked for two hours as she poured out her emotions and feelings.

"Rainbow, I want to be your woman."

"In my mind you are."

"No, what I'm saying is I'm willing to commit myself to only you."

"Just me?"

"Baby, I love you more than any man I've ever loved.

I feel so relaxed and safe with you, and I'd like us to spend the rest of our lives together."

"So are you proposing?"

"No silly, that's your job. I'm just saying that I choose to be your one and only."

"I accept," I deadpanned.

Cassandra shoved me playfully then kissed me on the lips. An elderly white woman passed, commenting on what a nice couple we made. Acknowledging thanks, we got in the truck and went to my place.

I turned Iceberg loose in the back yard then joined her in the house. Lifting two glasses from the cabinet, I mixed us potent brandy separators and led her to the living room. We sat on the sofa and Cassandra commented how nice it must be to have your own home.

My living room has a fireplace with a mantle above where I display trophies, family photos, and whatnots. On one side of the room is a floor-model television opposite an old component set I'd owned fifteen years so it held sentimental value and came complete with eight-track and turntable.

Most of my homeys were into CDs or cassettes and considered my album collection obsolete. I had begun to assemble a compact disk library, which took up less space, but since I didn't own a player I was just wasting money. Cassandra found it incredible that I was so far behind the times. To me she sounded like a salesperson.

"Baby, with a CD player the sound quality is much better and they don't scratch or break as easily as records. You can also go directly to any song you want to hear any time you want to, not to mention the space you'll save from those albums cluttering up the floor. I know what I'm getting you for Christmas."

"You talk as if my system is a dinosaur."

"It *is* ancient. I think you need a woman's touch with your decorating too, Mister Jordan," she smiled.

"I call it practical."

"Frugal is more like it," she couldn't control her giggles.

"Well, since I'm so old-fashioned, I'll do what squares do on a Friday night," I said.

"And what would that be?"

"I'll watch the news then go to bed."

"Do you have a grandmotherly gown for me? And some knitting yarn?"

We both cracked up while I flicked on the tube. The top story on the newscast was about a deadly gun battle at Eastmont Mall. They classified it as a drug deal gone bad. Sitting up, we focused our full attention on the anchorman.

He reported that the murders were part of a budding turf war between rival gangs in the city. They showed pictures, the first being Alphonse Malone. I knew him through Stoney. They'd never had a rift because each controlled his part of town.

Next they showed his bodyguard, a guy named Tyrone. We knew him as Big T and always felt that he would die a violent death because that's the life he lived. Then they showed a dude I'd never seen before, but Cassandra jumped up and shouted, "THAT'S EARL!"

"Who?"

"Baby, that's Earl Robinson — he hangs out with Buckey and Violet!"

Before I could question her further, my body went numb. There in the center of the screen was my brother's picture, with the reporter yakking that the killings were in retaliation for his death.

Seeing this, I felt it would only be a matter of time before five-o came looking for me. They already thought I knew more than I'd let on, and now with tonight's killings they had to conclude I was in it up to my neck.

"Come on baby, let's go," I stated forcefully.

"Go where?"

"To your place."

I grabbed a change of clothing with urgency, filled Iceberg's food and water bowls with enough to last for a few days, and bounced with the quickness. Cassandra drove while I explained my reasoning for not wishing to be home. She didn't understand because she knew we were together all day. That being the case, she felt the police couldn't possibly suspect me.

"Yes they can, baby, because in their mind they figure you'll cover for me since you're my woman."

"They can think what they want," she bristled. "I know the truth."

Neither of us noticed the unmarked police car following our every move. The rollers had put a tail on me, and I didn't even know it. Parking in front of her crib, we went in. I plopped down on the couch, trying to make sense out of all the craziness going on.

15
NOBODY SAW NUTHIN'

Johnson and Hernandez stood in the mall's parking lot surveying the grisly murder scene. Uniformed officers roped off the entrance with patrol cars littering the landscape, their lights flashing wildly.

Ambulances, fire engines, and the coroner's wagon were all parked near the scene but far enough away to avoid contaminating any evidence. Reporters and photographers were busy interviewing anyone who spoke as if they had the slightest idea why the killings had occurred. Of course, all the information they received was pure speculation.

Before the detectives could do their job, microphones, flashbulbs, and questions bombarded them. They attempted to avoid it, but news people had deadlines to meet and were relentless in their approach. Without quotes from an official spokesperson, their story would be missing a crucial element.

The first thing journalists learn in school is that for any story you have to cover the five W's and an H, which is Who, What, When, Where, Why, and How. The Why is always provided by the police in a crime story and is normally given after an investigation is complete, but the media wanted answers immediately. Being the top-ranking official on the scene, Johnson was responsible for keeping the media informed.

"Detective Johnson, can we have a statement?" someone inquired.

"We will make a statement after the investigation has been completed."

"Is there any truth to the rumor that these killings were in retaliation for the Jordan murder Wednesday?" another asked.

"I'm not at liberty to divulge that information."

"Is this the beginning of a drug war?"

"Ladies and gentlemen, I'll be glad to make a statement after all the evidence has been gathered and examined. Now if you'll excuse me ..."

Johnson bulled through the horde of media personnel. Hernandez had already begun taking reports from the first officers on the scene. He also questioned maintenance staff working inside. They'd noticed the bodies while dumping trash and placed the call to 911. Of course, they hadn't witnessed anything.

"What we got, Manny?"

"Not much, Nate — nobody knows nothing."

"The victims?"

"Three. Alphonse Malone, head of the east-side empire,

along with his enforcer Tyrone Carter, alias Big T. The third guy is named Earl Robinson, master thief and con artist. All three have extensive criminal records. Oh, one more thing, Robinson was known to associate with James 'Spodie' McKnight."

"Any evidence?"

"Yes, we found a high-powered rifle with a scope on the ramp over there." Hernandez pointed to Slack's hiding place. "It was wiped clean of prints."

"There was only one weapon used?"

"We're not sure, Nate. Carter had a weapon in his hand, but we'll have to wait for the coroner's report."

"See if we can get a priority on it."

"I've already requested it, partner."

"What about our tail on Rainbow?"

"He's clean — been holed up with his woman all day. He did take a stroll around the lake at about the time these killings were committed."

"That guy knows something, Manny. After we leave here, I think we need to pay Mister Rainbow a visit. I have a gut feeling he knows who's behind these killings, and it's eating me up inside."

One thing about cops is that if they have a hunch, they'll play it out until becoming satisfied it means nothing. In Johnson's mind, I had information he needed to solve four murders, and he would have me shadowed until I told him what I knew, made a stupid move, or he solved the case on his own.

The two detectives spent the next hour talking with crime lab technicians, looking at the dead bodies from different angles, searching for clues, and brainstorming. The heat was on them to produce suspects before all-out war broke loose in the city.

Hopping in their service vehicle, they returned to headquarters to sift through the information gathered. They wanted to develop a profile of possible suspects bold enough to carry out crimes of this nature.

After writing their reports they walked to Mexicali Rose for dinner. Johnson ordered the usual super burrito, while Hernandez asked for a beef and cheese quesadilla. They reviewed the facts while waiting for their meal.

"Okay, Manny — Jordan, the biggest dealer on the west side, is murdered and robbed. One of the suspects, McKnight, is bludgeoned to death the same night. Jordan's brother Rainbow is caught red-handed at the scene the next day."

"With an airtight alibi," Manny interrupted.

"Eddie Turner (whose credibility is suspect) pins Stoney's murder on Henderson. Slack has been accused of eight murders but never charged. Two days later one of McKnight's associates, Earl Robinson, is executed along with the biggest dealer on the east side, plus his bodyguard. Through it all, the north-side boys have been silent. Both dealers were picked clean of drugs, cash, and jewels."

"It seems like someone is robbing dealers, Nate."

"That's exactly what's going on."

"Well, why are you on edge, partner?"

"Here's why, Manny — you have a law-abiding, hardworking citizen ..."

"Rainbow," Manny said without hesitation.

"Yes, and he finds McKnight dead *before* we do. I feel whoever else is involved, he probably knows their identity too. I also wonder what he would have done had he found McKnight alive."

"Why do you say that?" Manny answered Nate's question with one of his own.

"Because, Manny, you're an only child so you wouldn't think this way, but I have three brothers so I know the feeling."

"What feeling is that?"

"Well, if someone killed one of my brothers and I knew who did it, I'd search for them too."

"And when you found them?"

"They'd be six feet under," Johnson stated with conviction.

"See, Nate, that's where you read me wrong."

"How's that?"

"If somebody fucked with anyone in my family, I'd turn vigilante in a second. I don't need to have brothers or sisters to feel that way. I know Rainbow loves his brother, but his brother was a dope dealer selling poison and making more in a day than we make in a week. He died the way he lived, which is what I call equal justice," Manny whispered forcefully.

The waitress brought their food, and like every night, they ate in silence. Once finished, they headed to Cassandra's house.

16
A HELPING HAND

Cassandra sat on the sofa holding my hand as we discussed events of the past three days. The doorbell rang so she got up to answer it. Peering through the peephole, she turned to me whispering that it was the police. I motioned for her to open it and let them in. It was Johnson and Hernandez. As soon as she closed the door, I spoke.

"I heard about the shooting, but I had nothing to do with it."

"We know," Johnson replied.

Cassandra returned to her spot next to me while Johnson sat on the loveseat. Hernandez remained standing. I couldn't believe what I'd just heard.

"Wait a minute," I said, "if you know I had nothing to do with it, then what do you want with me?"

"We just want to talk."

"About what?"

"Look, Rainbow, we feel you may have information that could possibly assist us in breaking this case wide open. We came hoping you would cooperate."

"What do you want me to do?"

"Just tell me what you know," Johnson spoke softly.

"Okay, I know my brother was robbed and killed. Fact, I know fat Spodie drove the getaway car. Fact, I was wrongfully accused of his murder."

I slapped the back of my right hand into the palm of my left on each fact for emphasis. Johnson looked intently as I spoke, while Hernandez jotted notes on his pad.

"Fact, there were four people involved in Stoney's killing. Fact, Earl was Spodie's homeboy and now he's dead. Fact, Alphonse had no beef with my brother. Fact, Spodie and Earl hang around with some fool named Buckey who ambushed me right outside this door the night Ricky was killed."

"Hold on," Hernandez said, "who is Buckey?" He resumed writing.

"Buckey's real name is Curtis Jones," Cassandra answered.

"You know him?" Johnson asked her.

"Yes, he's my ex-husband's brother."

"Where does he live?" they asked in unison.

"I have the address in my phone book — let me go get it."

Cassandra went into the bedroom to get her phone book while we waited patiently. She returned with the address written on a stick-um memo and handed it to Hernandez.

"What else can you tell us about Jones?" Johnson asked her.

"He's crazy, always involved in criminal activity."

"Give me a description of him."

"He's about five feet nine, weighs maybe a hundred and eighty pounds, always wears his hair in cornrows, has a mustache, goatee, big lips, yellow teeth, stinks, and is dark as midnight."

"How did he know Rainbow?"

"He didn't. I think he pays my neighbor to tell him about any man I see. He has a stupid notion that me and his brother will get back together once he's released."

"Released from where?" Hernandez asked, writing furiously.

"He's in San Quentin"

"What's your ex-husband's name?"

"Calvin Jones — they call him Shakey."

"Do you know Robert Henderson — they call him Slack?"

"No, I don't. I couldn't stand Buckey or his friends. At first Calvin worked and wouldn't fool with them, then he started hanging around those thugs every day. Not to mention skirt chasing, so I divorced him."

"Rainbow, how did you find out about McKnight being involved in your brother's death?"

"I know someone who saw it go down — he didn't see the people but recognized Spodie's car. I was just going over to his house to ask him if he'd loaned his ride to any-body that night. I also wanted to see his reaction."

"Is there anything else you can tell us?"

"No, that just about covers it — what about you, baby?"

"That's it," Cassandra said.

"Well, we thank you for your assistance."

Johnson rose to leave, then he and Hernandez shook our hands. We showed them to the door, and I felt as though a ton of bricks had been lifted off my shoulders. Suddenly a thought occurred to me.

"Sargeant Johnson ... " They both turned around. " ... How did you two find me?"

"We've had you tailed since your release this morning," he smiled wickedly.

"Well I'll be damned." I shook my head, grinning.

As Cassandra shut the door, we saw Nadine's curtain close abruptly. Laughing, we hugged each other and went to bed.

17
DON'T CROSS ME

Slack dropped Buckey off at Earl and Brenda's crib then sped off. He and Yolanda would have a cool time tonight. He still felt that Buckey should have given him the pistol to dispose of because guns were his specialty. Since Buckey refused, that would be his problem to worry about. Buckey walked up to the door and knocked.

"Where's Earl, baby?" she asked, looking out the door.

"He dead," Buckey stated matter of factly.

"Dead?" She didn't believe what she heard.

"Da deal went bad, lot of shootin took place, Earl got hit."

Brenda was stunned. She just saw Earl less than one hour ago. Guilt gripped her heart as tears poured freely from her eye sockets. The fact that he died angry at her caused even more pain.

Buckey wrapped his arms around her waist as tears continued to flow. The tighter he held, the drier her eyes became, replaced by a raging fire in her body. Lifting her head up, she gave him a hungry kiss, which was salty from her teardrops. Buckey became aroused but his brain flashed a warning signal.

First, if they had sex right now he'd be there for a few hours. Second, since five-o would be coming around to give her the bad news, he didn't want to be anywhere near the place. Third and most important was after every job, he always went straight home. Violet would know something wasn't right, then he'd have hell on his hands.

"Look, baby," he began, "da police gone be comin round heah ta tell you what happened ta Earl. When dey do, act like it's da first time you heard about it." She nodded so he continued, "Don't say nuthin bout me to da pigs, don't even mention mah name, you got dat?"

"Yes, I got it," she said solemnly.

"Ah'mo call you in da moanin so you be waitin fa da call, okay?"

"I'll be here."

"Lock dis doe and remembah, act like you don't know Earl been dead."

Buckey gave her a kiss along with a powerful hug then bounced. Brenda slumped down on the sofa, not knowing whether to laugh or cry. On the one hand, the door was now open for her to build a relationship with Buckey. On the other, she did love Earl even though he slept around. He brought money to the home, unlike some of the losers she made a habit of choosing. The thought of Buckey having a woman never crossed her mind.

She knew nothing about him yet had fallen madly in love. Women fall in love daily because a man drops the bomb in bed, while men simply consider it good sex. Brenda had always been a fool for men, but this time she went overboard. A rude awakening was all she would receive.

Buckey drove home not knowing if Brenda would play it off in front of five-o or run her mouth. Realizing that he knew nothing about her caused him to worry. All of a sudden she didn't seem that appealing anymore.

If Violet discovered his secret she would probably kill the girl and never trust him again. Now he felt foolish for stupidly risking a good thing with Violet. He pulled in the driveway and trudged slowly into the crib.

"Honey, is that you?" Violet called out from the kitchen.

"Yeah, it's me."

"Did everything go smoothly?"

"Naw, we had a shootout."

"What happened?" she asked while drying her hands.

"Dose foos tried ta rough me up, den Slack blew dey ass away."

"Well, it's good y'all didn't get hurt."

"Earl's dead."

"Baby, Earl got killed?"

"Yeah, he got kilt — da niggah wadn't no help no way, stannin dare like a dumb ass."

OAKTOWN DEVIL

"He didn't help?" she took a seat, wide-eyed.

"Hell, naw. Okay, dis how it went, dat foo Tonio was talkin shit so ah put 'im in check."

"Know that's right."

"Den dis big ugly-ass niggah grabbed mc an try ta rough me up but Slack popped 'im wit a cap."

"Right on, Slack," Violet said proudly.

"Now when Slack popped 'im, ah bum-rushed dat ass-hole Tonio. Awight, we start rasslin an ah was bout ta get his ass when ah tripped over Earl."

"Wait a minute, baby, how you trip on Earl if he was standing up?"

"Da lass thang dat clown Tee done was shoot Earl, so he was stumblin roun an got in da way."

"Damn."

"When ah fell over Earl, da gun flied out mah hand an Tonio picked it up, so ah ducked behind da truck an Slack blew his ass ta hell. Den ah took his shit an we cut out."

Buckey pulled out the loot for Violet to see then continued, "Since Slack bailed mah ass propah, ah kicked 'im down half a dis cause if he would'na been dare, mah ass woulda been grass."

"Slack came through," Violet stated truthfully.

"Yeah, he did. Earl didn't even wont him ta go but ah tole 'im where we was gone be."

"Good for you, baby."

"See, ah got mo sense den Earl gave me credit foe — he don't know how ta cover his back but ah damn show do, shidd."

154

"What you gone do now?"

"Lay low. Da police don't know nuttin but ah'mo make mahself scarce anyway."

"Go lie down, baby, I'll be upstairs in a minute."

"Somethin look different in heah."

"Nothin's different, I just cleaned up." She kissed him.

Their house was always filthy, so now that it was clean, it appeared that something was strange. Buckey trudged up the stairs and fell across the bed. Violet came up a minute later, stripped down naked, then proceeded to undress him. After making love they fell asleep wrapped in each other's arms.

Three hours later Buckey woke up and dressed, telling Violet that he was headed to the store for beer. Once he bounced she put on a gown and went downstairs for dinner.

She had prepared a nice meal of meatloaf, mashed potatoes, and gravy. On the side she had tossed salad with lettuce, tomatoes, bean sprouts, red cabbage, cucumbers, red onions, mushrooms, and diced chicken topped with ranch dressing.

Violet sat at the table and started eating, only to be interrupted by loud knocking at her door. She peered through the windowpane, spotting two suited police officers.

"May I help you?"

"Yes ma'am, I'm Sargeant Johnson and this is my partner Sargeant Hernandez." They flashed their badges.

"Is there something wrong?"

"We're looking for Curtis Jones. Is he here?"

"No, he isn't. You wanna tell me what this is about?"

"We have a few questions we'd like to ask him. Does he live here?"

"He comes here sometimes — I wouldn't call it living here," Violet lied.

"Well, if you see him, ask him to call me — it's very important." Johnson slid his card through the door.

"Look, I'm his fiancee so I have a right to know what you want with my man."

"Ma'am, it doesn't concern you, just tell him to call me."

Buckey hit the block in his hooptie, and upon seeing the detectives at his front door drove right by. He was so enraged that he started talking to himself.

"Dat bitch done gave dem mah name, ah'mo kill her. Da stupid-ass hoe done moufed ta five-o, ah never shoulda start fuckin wif dat punk-ass bitch. Ah'ma hafta check her ass right now."

He drove to Brenda's home in a rage, deciding he would have to put a zip on her lip. His plan was just beginning to take shape, so he couldn't afford to let a square chick like her screw it up.

Parking down the block, he surveyed the set. Satisfied that no cops were staking out her pad, he jogged around the corner, cut through an adjacent complex, scaled the fence and knocked on her door.

Since receiving the news of Earl's death, Brenda had done plenty of soul-searching. She loved the way Buckey made her feel but really didn't know him. What she did know, she did not like.

He had lousy vocabulary, poor hygiene, rotten teeth,

and showed no remorse about Earl's murder. She would not feel comfortable taking him around her friends. By contrast, Earl had style, excellent grooming habits, and blended in at any function.

Panic struck when she remembered telling Buckey she was his. What if he took her up on it? Just as she decided to tell him they could not be together, her doorbell rang.

Flicking on the porch light while looking through the peephole, she saw it was none other than Buckey. Knots formed in her stomach as she opened the door and stepped aside.

"Oh, ah cain't get a kiss now?" he asked.

"It's not that, I'm just drained."

"Well, you kissed me all da other times."

"Look, man, what do you want?"

Buckey was taken aback by her disposition. He looked in her bathroom, bedroom, and linen closet. Seeing no cops caused his tension to ease, but he wasn't done. Whipping out his gun, he wiped it clean of prints and hid it under some towels.

"What are you looking for?" she asked, clearly irked by his actions.

"Ah'm jus makin show nobody's heah wif you."

"'Wif you'," she muttered sarcastically.

"Look, bitch, dis ain't no game."

"Buckey, what are you talking about? You done got my man killed, now you're snooping around my home calling me out my name — what's your problem?"

"Ah ain't got no problem cept dis gun." He pointed where he'd just hid it.

"What gun?" She came to look.

"Dis gun." He handed it to her.

"That's not mine." She dropped it in disgust.

"If it ain't yours den why it's in yo crib?"

"Look, you're gonna have to leave."

"Oh, you tell da police bout me den wont me ta leave, huh?"

"Tell the police about you? Man, you sick."

Buckey rared back and slugged her with a vicious blow to the jaw. Brenda dropped like a sack of potatoes. Scrambling to her feet, she charged at him with fingernails clawing.

"Motherfucker, don't nobody be hitting on me, you dirty bastard!"

Buckey dropped her with another right, causing blood to pour from her nose. Having never been hit by a man, she didn't understand why he used her as a punching bag. Fear gripped her.

Jumping on her before she had time to move, Buckey rained blows to her face. She tried to cover up as this lunatic pounded her into submission. His emotions overflowed as he beat her down.

To him the worst thing a person could do was sick five-o on someone else. Brenda attempted to scream, but he clutched her throat with both hands blocking her vocal cords. No sound came out, yet she struggled with all her might.

Buckey couldn't secure a tight grip because her neck was as thick as her thighs. Plus she kicked, scratched, and writhed all over the floor. The blood flowing from her nose seeped into her mouth, causing her to gag.

Using every ounce of strength with her life depending on it, she threw him off. Her face was a bloody mess and she had trouble breathing, but Buckey didn't care. Jumping to his feet, he kicked her ribs savagely, breaking two in the process.

He stomped her face, head, and thighs then dropped to his knees and choked the life out of her. The tighter his clamp got, the less resistance she supplied. Feces spilled from her body as death overtook it.

Buckey continued choking even after Brenda was dead. Once he knew the mission was accomplished he got up, brushed himself off, and calmly walked out the door. Leaping the fence and running to his car, he drove home.

CELEBRATE THE
GOOD TIMES

Slack arrived home animated, which was normal when he scored big. Yolanda knew from his actions that he was in the money. Bursting through the door, he gave her a kiss then put away his weapons. He returned to the living room boasting like a millionaire.

"Baby, get dressed, I'm taking you to Sweet Jimmie's."

"Oh yeah?" she said, amused.

"Hell yeah, I'm takin my woman out tonight."

"And how, Mister Henderson, will you pay for this grand evening, with your looks?"

"No," he said, handing her the ropes. "Try these on for size."

"Baby, are these for me?" Yolanda was excited now.

"I told you, nothing but the best for my wife."

Yolanda put on the ropes, modeling them in her bathroom mirror. She'd never owned anything fancier than costume jewelry, so this had to be a big heist. One thing she knew was that when her man acted stupid, he had a pocket full of scrill. Slack handed her eighteen c-notes, grinning while she counted.

Yolanda went in the bedroom and stashed the money under the carpet, placing a nightstand on top. If someone found her scrill, they would have to tear up her bedroom to do it.

"Baby, you did good."

She grabbed Slack in a bear hug, kissing his lips passionately. The eighteen tonight along with the thirteen from Stoney had their bank fat. Slack only kept two hundred from his jobs because he knew Yolanda was better at managing money.

She supplied his smokes, weed, booze, and grub, so he only needed cash for gas, oil, and pocket change. If left to handle the funds, he'd blow it partying and drinking with his homeys. Upon returning home he'd have to fight an angry Yolanda for being stupid.

The cash they'd acquired from Stoney and Tonio would last a year. Yolanda would pinch twenty or forty at a time for household needs, never taking large amounts. Her welfare check and food stamps always lasted the entire month because she was frugal and a good homemaker.

A typical meal of neck bones, red beans, rice, and corn bread would cost five bucks yet feed their family of six with everyone stuffed. There would also be leftovers for the teens returning from late-night escapades.

Yolanda cooked hearty soul-food meals daily and could have provided the welfare agency with a perfect blueprint for recipients. The few bills were paid on the first of the month and meals planned in the same manner as a dining hall.

She could tell you today what they would have for dinner two weeks later. Giving Slack an all-too-familiar look, she kissed him hungrily then headed for the bedroom. Glancing over her shoulder, she whispered in a husky voice, "Come get it."

Grinning sheepishly like a child receiving praise, he followed. Slack loved having sex with his wife because after four kids it was a luxury. She only gave it up when she didn't have a "headache" or they didn't fight. He knew if he kept having weeks like this, his dipstick would be checking her oil level on a regular maintenance schedule.

Yolanda was huge and ugly but very good in bed. She would let him bump-n-grind, matching each and every stroke. Once he orgasmed, she locked his skinny frame in a vice grip and bucked like a bronco. Slack felt like a cowboy trying not to fall off a steer. By the time 'Lon was done, he was totally drained. Rolling over, he dozed off while she reached for a cigarette and lit up.

He was the only man she had ever had intercourse with and she loved him to the core. Her body was her personal shrine, and she was not about to spread it thin. The few men bold enough to make a pass were cursed out royally, the persistent ones challenged to a fist fight.

She put on her house robe and went to take a bath. Next she washed her dishes and placed leftovers in the fridge. While cleaning, she wondered what the police wanted with her man. She wasn't concerned because Slack always covered his tracks.

However, she still hated that Fric n Frac had the nerve to come looking. Turning out the lights, she joined her man in bed and drifted off into a peaceful sleep.

19
DON'T DO NUTHIN'
STUPID

Buckey parked in the Acorn lot, scanning the block to see if five-o watched. With the coast clear, he sprinted across the street through two yards. As he entered the back door, Violet hung up the telephone.

"Who was dat on da phone?"

"That was Nadine. She said the police were at Cassandra's house questioning that dude she messing with."

"What dey wont?"

"She didn't say. She did say that when they were leaving, all four of 'em was laughing and stuff."

"Das all she said?"

"No, she said Cassandra's friend asked them how did they find him and they told him they had him tailed."

"You think dey tole um bout me?"

"Probably, because after you beat him up, you know Cassandra told him who you was."

"Dat don't mean nuttin."

"Buckey, he was at Spodie's house the next day, so whoever told him about that probably told him about us, too."

"Ah don't give a shit bout no probly, ah'm of da mine ta go kill his ass."

"Baby, listen to me, the police ain't got nothin — they searching for straws, but if you make a mistake, then they gone get you."

"Yeah," he stroked his goatee, "dey waitin foe me ta make a mistake."

"Just don't do nothin stupid. I think you should stop slangin rocks for a few days since they're looking for you."

"Why you say dat?"

"Damn, Buckey, think." She pointed to her temple. "If they find you and you got a pocket full of dope, they got yo ass."

"Yeah, ah guess you right."

"I know I'm right. How you get those scratches on your neck?"

"It's a long story."

"Buckey, tell me," she insisted.

"When ah went ta git Earl, he had tole his woman what we was gone do, so when Slack dropped me back off at mah ride, ah went in da house ta tell her what happened. Ah tole her dat when da police come an say Earl was dead, don't mention mah name. She said cool. Den when ah went to da stowe an saw da police ax you some questions, ah thought she done said Earl was wif me, so ah went back over dare. She opened da doe den start talkin crazy, callin me stupid an shit. So since ah couldn't trust her ta keep her mouf shut, ah choked her ta death. She was scratchin an shit but ah zipped her lip forever, den ah came back home."

"That's why you came through the back?"

"Naw, ah did dat jus in case da pigs was watchin da front."

Violet pondered his statement before speaking. "I guess you did the right thing."

"Hell yeah, ah did da rite thang. We don't know what she liable ta say, so ah made sho she don't say nuttin *no moe.*" He emphasized the last point.

"Come on, baby, let's go lie down."

She took his hand, leading him to the bedroom. Buckey felt relieved knowing that Violet understood, but deep down he thought maybe Brenda didn't deserve to die. More than likely Rainbow and Cassandra sent the police.

As he followed Violet upstairs he thought about the wonderful sex Brenda had given, which caused his manhood to swell full of blood. If only she hadn't talked so crazy he wouldn't have had to kill her.

Violet turned to face him and noticed his sweatpants poking out. A large smile creased her face as her robe hit the floor. Cupping her big breasts in her hands, she gazed starry-eyed at her man.

"Is that for me?" she cooed.

"If you wont it."

She gripped his pole and led him to the bed by it. Buckey kicked off his shoes, pulling down his sweats and underwear just enough to expose his rod. Without foreplay or anything, he rammed it home, tearing into her like there was no tomorrow.

Violet closed her eyes, moaning in rhythm, which spurred him to stroke harder. The louder she got, the deeper he went. Buckey closed his eyes and imagined that he was screwing Brenda. Thinking about how she yelled and screamed only made him plow into Violet more fiercely.

He knew this was special for his woman because she hadn't moaned like this in years. His penis filled with blood, erupting like a volcanic explosion inside her steaming hole.

Feeling his hot liquid suffusing her womb triggered an orgasm so powerful it caused his meat to stiffen again. Buckey rolled her on her belly, driving it home doggie-style repeatedly.

She clutched the sheets, allowing him any liberty he chose with her willing body. It felt as though he were tearing the lining out, but she didn't care because the only man capable of sending her over the edge was Buckey.

He squirted off a second load, collapsing on her back in the process. Rolling over he pulled off his clothes and fell asleep instantly. Violet's body was on fire, setting off several mini-orgasms.

The next thirty minutes were spent with her gazing lovingly at her snoring man. He always gave good love after committing deadly crimes, but this time was different. This time he hit it like he would when they first got together.

She didn't know what but knew it had to be something about killing Earl's woman that caused him to fuck her the way he did tonight. She didn't really care either, because in her mind she'd put him to sleep with a smile on his face. Thoroughly satisfied, Violet rolled over and dozed off.

The next morning they woke up and agreed to get out of Oaktown. Getting in the car, they took 580 to Pleasanton and the fair. The circuit operated two-week runs from county to county, ending in Sacramento with the grand finale, the state fair.

Even though they could also go to Vallejo or San Mateo, Oaktowners tended to choose Pleasanton, over the hills to the east.

At the fair the smell of bar-b-que, corn dogs, popcorn, cotton candy, and other specialty items permeated the air. They had the usual assortment of rides such as ferris wheels, bumper cars, air swings, roller coasters, and spinning tops where the floor dropped beneath your feet. Buckey and Violet rode each one, enjoying the rides tremendously.

He was like a kid walking around with a fist full of tickets, getting upset when he had to wait in line. After the carousel they headed for the games of chance.

Buckey started at the hoop challenge, which looked easy enough when employees did it. However, every shot he attempted missed the mark badly. He didn't care because he was having fun.

Violet pitched dimes for dishes, glasses, and ashtrays.

She would purchase ten dimes for a dollar then wildly toss them all at once. After spending thirty dollars she won six glasses that could have been purchased for less than four bucks in a store.

Buckey got hooked on the rifle game where you fill a balloon with water until it bursts. Winning small plastic toys, he continued playing and trading them in for larger prizes. By the time he finished he had won a giant stuffed animal at a cost of fifty dollars. He still considered himself a winner.

They spent money on everything from gangster photos to buttons, t-shirts, and sketches. Next they headed to the buildings and got suckered into buying carpet cleaner, beef jerky, knives, and window cleaner.

Buckey tried to show up the demonstrators with his wit, but most people observing secretly hoped he'd shut up. Getting their hands stamped, Buckey and Violet went to the car to put away their winnings and purchases. Sitting down at a picnic bench, they dined on cheese steak sandwiches, curly fries, and beer.

"What you wanna do now, babe?" he asked.

"I want to go to the amphitheater and watch the bands."

"Aw, fuck dat, less go to da track."

Violet did not feel like arguing today so she agreed. Buckey stalked off towards the races, with her struggling to keep pace. He paid the admission and bought a program, racing form, and beer.

They headed to the paddock area where horses walked

in a circle led by helpers. Spectators looked the ponies over closely, trying to pick out any flaw or feature they thought could give them an advantage.

"See, da thang you look foe is which one is sweatin da most and who looks da strongest," Buckey said. "Come on, ah'm bout ta go make mah bets."

Violet stood by as he placed his wagers. Noticing all the losing tickets scattered on the ground, she thought to herself that Buckey didn't know what he was doing. He would probably be throwing away tickets too.

"Ah wont a five-dollah exacta, box 1, 2, 5, an play dat foe times."

"That'll be one hundred and twenty dollars," the ticket seller stated.

Buckey peeled off six twenties then told Violet, "Less go watch da race."

"Buckey, why you bet so much?"

"Cause you gotta spend money ta win money."

"How much you gonna win?"

"I'ont know, it depends on da odds. Ah got some long-shots so when ah win, we gone get paid." He laughed loudly.

The race started, with fans yelling for their selections. Violet was amused by all the craziness going on around her. People were screaming, urging their horses on, while Buckey watched intently. His attention was focused on the horses as the announcer called the race.

"Heading into the clubhouse turn it's I'm a Big Believer followed closely by Jamonit with She's So Fine two lengths behind."

"See baby, if any two uh mah three come in first an second, we win," Buckey screamed above the noisy crowd.

"Coming down the backstretch, it's I'm a Big Believer battling neck and neck with Jamonit. I'm a Big Believer is doing all he can to hold off the charge. It's Jamonit, I'm a Big Believer. I'm a Big Believer, Jamonit. I'm a Big Believer . . . in front."

Buckey slapped the program into the palm of his hand, grinning broadly, then gave Violet a kiss.

"Less go get mah money," he said. "I'm a big baleavah ta jam on it, shidd, dey cain't fuck wit me, shidd," he stated proudly.

"Baby, why ain't nobody in line?" Violet asked as they approached the windows.

"Cause dem foos bet da favorite."

The payoff was posted with numbers one and five on the exacta ticket returning nine hundred dollars for a five-dollar bet.

"Nine muthafuckin hundred, yeah!" Buckey hollered.

Violet's face beamed with pride. Since Buckey had bet four times instead of once, their take was a cool thirty-six hundred. Violet was beside herself.

"Baby, show me how to do this!" she said enthusiastically.

"Naw, you wanna go watch da bands."

"Not no moe — I wanna win some money."

Buckey laughed so hard tears fell from his eyes. Violet grabbed the program from him, attempting to study it without a clue as to what she was doing. He regained his composure and began explaining everything he knew about horse racing, failing to mention that no matter how scientific you got, it was still luck. She hung on every word as if he were a genius.

They played three more races without winning a thing. Buckey told her she broke his concentration. Amazed at how five dollars could return such a huge profit, Violet vowed to learn this game. It wasn't like the lottery or slot machines, which were pure luck; with this game you chose your own picks then watched the horses run. It all seemed so simple.

After the races they watched the bands anyway. Violet could not remember spending a day this pleasurable with her man. The entire day had been nothing but fun, and she wished they could do things like this more often. Exhausted, they got in the car and headed home.

20
FAMILY AFFAIR

My job was to make sure we had a spot for our family picnic. Cassandra woke me up at six in the morning, giving me time to freshen up. Momma went to church on Sundays, so our picnic would be held this year on Saturday the third of July. Stopping at the crib, I picked up my bar-b-que pit along with Iceberg. Grabbing my newspaper off the front porch, I bounced.

Dimond Park is one of the prettiest spots in Oaktown. Its serene setting and picturesque view make the place a choice picnic ground. There are several entrances to the park, the main one being on Fruitvale. The park's true beauty isn't apparent here. Instead, the first thing you see are the tennis courts located to the left, encased in a twenty-foot-high chain-link fence. To the right is a steep hill covered with dirt, and directly above that a wooden fence separates the park from the beautiful homes adorning the neighborhood.

A gravel walking trail leads directly into the heart of the park. Here you find a very large picnic area surrounded by huge trees and luscious greenery. The main area has several tables plus a few fire pits. Scattered throughout are additional tables, benches, and more pits.

The children's sandbox is complemented by monkey bars, swings, slide, and the usual assortment of tunnels. Right behind sit the restrooms, which always reek of urine. The hand dryers never work and toilets stayed clogged with litter.

Hoop courts are next to the restrooms, with three-on-three games taking place regularly. However, the talent level isn't that high, since serious hoopsters take their game to Mosswood, located on the north side.

Another large patch of grass is situated near the courts, directly in front of the swimming pool. A creek flows through, from Montclair all the way to the flatlands.

On a raised platform with overhanging trees, the pool operates year round, the prettiest facility in town. Above that is a parking lot and recreation center. The only way you can drive into Dimond by auto is to take MacArthur two blocks north of Fruitvale. There you turn right and drive down a narrow winding road.

I took this route inside the park to claim my spot. Uncle Jeff was there waiting and had roped off our section. He expected me, but I was pleasantly surprised to see him. Uncle Jeff wasn't actually related but was Mom's lifelong friend. He had no children of his own, yet treated all his "nieces and nephews" better than most of their parents treated them.

A bar-b-que master, his method was exquisite. He formed a pile with the coals then lit them and watched as they burned ash-gray. Lightly setting the grill in place, he scraped it clean and wiped the residue off with newspaper.

Using a twisted coat hanger, he poked and moved the coals until they were spread out evenly. Jeff came prepared with meat from Momma's, seasoned and ready for grilling.

Momma outdid herself, as usual, supplying ten slabs of pork ribs along with six of beef. She also included two humongous bags of chicken wings, plus hot dogs, links, burger patties, and a case of ribeye steaks.

Uncle Jeff stood a meager five ten but weighed more than two hundred pounds. His button-down shirt overlapped his trousers in order to camouflage his beer gut. He wore polyester slacks with outdated shoes, but Uncle Jeff was presentable. Forever with a brim on his dome to hide a receding hairline, he gave the impression of an old guy trying to be young.

His facial appearance resembled a rat, which ironically is what Pearlie Mae and some of their other friends called him. It was a nickname they'd given him as a child that stuck. Of course, we always had to address him as Uncle Jeff, but as we grew older "Rat" became acceptable to him. The word didn't sound right leaving my mouth so I kept on calling him Uncle Jeff.

He drank beer twenty-four/seven, and when he didn't

have one you'd ask if everything was okay. Employed as a custodian at Cal Berkeley for thirty-five years, Uncle Jeff would talk your head off about mopping and shit. Because he often rehashed the same boring tales with predictable endings, we knew each story by heart. If you had the ignorance or the nerve to call him a janitor instead of a custodian, you could kiss the next hour and a half goodbye.

Uncle Jeff placed three slabs of ribs on the pit, watching like a hawk while downing the first of what would be many beers today. Just as the fire flamed up he covered it with the lid and opened the top vent. Five minutes later he turned the meat over and reached for his "mop." Since you damn near had to go to Texas to get a mop, Uncle Jeff created his own by nailing a loose-fitting towel onto a skinny stick. Every ten minutes he'd turn the meat over and baste it with his juice.

His mop juice was a combination of vinegar, pickle juice, liquid smoke, pepper, salt, garlic, and lemon slices. Sometimes he would heat it in a saucepan and add water or beer. Sometimes he would not. Uncle Jeff's ingredients changed according to his liquor intake, but by the time he finished mopping, turning, and slow-cooking his meat, you would be eating some of the tastiest ribs you ever had.

At nine o'clock I left Uncle Jeff and Iceberg then went home to shower and change clothes. I put on a black sweatsuit with matching sneakers and t-shirt. Hopping in Bertha, I cruised Foothill, pulling up in front of Sherry's.

Located at Seminary and MacArthur across from Baskin-Robbins, Sherry's is where I go for haircuts. Sandwiched neatly between a pizzeria and nail shop, the place is clean and colorful.

The large interior has at least twenty hair dryers perched atop cushioned chairs. There are five beauticians, four barbers, fifteen seats in the waiting area, and a supply counter where you purchase everything from incense to nail polish. Two twenty-seven-inch color televisions are bolted to the ceiling, giving everyone a good view.

Another attention-grabber is the youthful energy of the place. Most of the employees appear to be teenagers but are much older. You would not know who Sherry is until someone calls out her name. Her age is a mystery, but she appears to be in her late twenties. She has a caramel complexion with long hair which today cascades down past her shoulders. Her style changes daily and nothing slips by her, because she watches all activity like a hawk.

After getting a cool cut and trim, I hopped in Bertha and headed for Cassandra's. When I arrived she was dressed and ready to go, wearing black stretch pants that hugged every curve and prominently displayed her butt. Complementing her outfit were black high heels along with a skin-tight halter top.

Dimond was packed, and with all my relatives in from out of town for Stoney's funeral it looked like we were having a family reunion. Parking on Fruitvale Avenue, Cassandra and I made our way to the family. As we passed kinfolk and strangers, Cassandra's butt was the center of attention. My cousin Billy from Vegas eased up to me whispering, "Cuz, you picked a winner dare, boy — baby got back. I know you be tearing that shit up."

"Billy, how ya doin?" We hugged, laughing.

I introduced Cassandra to everybody, then we went to eat. Uncle Jeff placed ribs on our plate smothered in sauce. I preferred his mop meat, but the sauce was his pride and joy. He'd combine ketchup, mustard, molasses, chopped garlic, lemon slices, hot sauce, beer, sugar, pepper, and salt, allowing it to simmer all day. The longer you waited before eating, the more flavorful his sauce would be. Cassandra tasted a sample and was sprung instantly.

Cousin Pat made the potato salad, while her man Richard took his usual hundred photographs. Drumming up support for his dry cleaning business, he'd point out every wrinkle in someone's attire. We always made sure our clothes were wrinkle-free when we knew he was coming.

Johnny Ray and Gerri brought the baked beans, Rodney and Elaine the drinks. Elaine did most of the cooking at house get-togethers, but park outings were not her thing. She and Rod would chaperone all the children to the swimming pool, enjoying themselves even more than the kids.

Rufus provided the boom box, along with more compact disks than we needed, while Maxine strutted around the park in her work uniform. Claiming she had to work overtime, I figured she would probably be accepting some new lover's penis before the day was over.

Auntie Pam and Uncle Randy sat with Pearlie Mae, rehashing memories from childhood. They were the center of attention, discussing in detail many of our dead relatives. Cousin Ronnie blessed the food before anyone took a bite. He was an ordained minister and would officiate

Stoney's funeral. Among the new breed of his profession, Ronnie was capable of fire and brimstone sermons but like many New Age pastors, he also dealt with the here and now.

Stoney's wife Sabrina sat looking dumbfounded with some clown by her side. She tried to pass him off as her cousin, but their body language suggested otherwise. One hour after making her entrance she excused herself, claiming that she had to attend her own family gathering.

Mary Jo, my shit-talking cousin from Vegas, was both phine and fast. Born and raised in Lost Wages (as she dubbed it), she considered Oaktown slow. This was due to the fact that Vegas is a fast town full of high rollers. She had to be physically restrained from mauling Sabrina and was extremely upset that the girl had the nerve to bring another man to her dead husband's family bar-b-que.

Rochelle provided a huge aluminum pan full of tossed salad, which was mostly lettuce. Fixing enough food to last herself and five crumb-snatchers two days, she openly stuffed it in her beat-up hooptie. She knew no one would complain for fear of creating a scene, and a scene she would provide if provoked.

At six Cassandra and I said our goodbyes then split. I handed Uncle Jeff a twenty, asking him to take my dog and pit to his home. Back at Cassandra's, we ate more food then went to bed. After sleeping in late Sunday morning, we went to my place for my truck.

Uncle Jeff lived on the north side, three blocks from Tech High. He owned a modest two-bedroom bungalow in a nice quiet neighborhood. After knocking repeatedly I went to the back and untied Iceberg. Securing the pit in the back of the truck, I smiled as Iceberg manned his normal spot.

Cassandra held my hand, snuggling under my arm as I took the street route home. We painted a pretty picture for the people riding behind us. I let Berg out and rolled my pit up the driveway. Cassandra began making omelettes while I opened three days' worth of mail. I sat down to eat, surprised that she had also prepared a small omelette for Iceberg, who wolfed it down with the quickness.

"Baby, this looks tasty," I said while drenching my food with hot sauce.

"I enjoy cooking for my man."

"So does this mean I can expect this on a regular basis?"

"Yes, honey, it does."

We ate, then she began tidying up the kitchen. The next thing I knew she gave my home a complete room-by-room cleaning. I was in the way, so she politely shoved me out the door to keep Berg company. When she finished her chores, we hit the bed and made love.

• • •

I woke at four and dressed in my black suit, then we went to Cassandra's so she could get dressed. Satisfied, we headed to Williams' for Stoney's quiet hour. The funeral home was packed, a testament to all the friends Stoney had come to know during his brief life.

Sitting in the front row with my family, I cried my eyes out while Cassandra rubbed my back. The organist played soft music, which caused tears to flow from most people in attendance.

When the service was over, I kissed Momma goodbye, telling her that we would see her tomorrow. When we got home, I shared my family photo album with Cassandra, along with filling her in on Stoney's life. Exhausted from the day's activities, we were preparing for bed when the phone rang.

"Hello," I greeted.

"Rainbow?" The voice was low and chilling.

"Yeah, who is this?"

"Don't matter."

"What you want, Don't Matter?"

"You a dead man," he said then hung up.

"Who was that?" asked Cassandra.

"Don't matter, let's get some sleep."

"Okay, baby."

We crawled into bed and Cassandra fell asleep as soon as her head hit the pillow. In the darkened room I stared at the ceiling as my mind raced for clues. I figured the call had to come from that fool Buckey and decided that after the funeral I would deal with him once and for all. Content with my plan, I dozed off.

21
BUSY OFF-DAY

Johnson and Hernandez reported for duty on Sunday, which was their normal day off. They had each received a call from Moroski and Colvin, the police officers investigating Brenda's murder.

John Moroski was a giant six-foot-six redneck with blond hair and blue eyes on a three-hundred-pound wide body. The suits he wore were always a size too small, and behind his back other officers dubbed him "Pumpkin."

Peter Colvin stood six four with red hair and brown eyes on a chiseled two hundred and sixty pounds. Moroski was the senior of the two, but these best friends treated each other as equals. They'd worked as a team for five years and lived on the same cul-de-sac in Walnut Creek.

Their families vacationed together, with each man's children referring to the other man as "uncle." Carpooling to work daily, they considered Oaktown the jungle, which is how many of their white associates also felt.

Each man would have left the force for better-paying, safer jobs but chose against it in order not to break up the team. Neither liked Johnson, feeling as if one day he would be their superior. Just the thought of taking orders from a nigger turned their stomachs.

Nate and Manny pulled up to the crime scene at Brenda's house. The usual assortment of squad cars, medical and coroner's staff, and media greeted their arrival. Tape roped off the area. Uniformed officers stood around joking while reporters waited impatiently nearby. Before they got a chance to bombard Johnson with questions, he conducted a brief press conference.

"We will not have a statement until all facts are in," he told the reporters, then went inside.

Brenda's body lay decomposed in the spot where Buckey had left it, with flies hovering around as the evidence techs went about their duties. They snapped photos, dusted for prints, outlined the prone figure with chalk, and searched for clues. The gun was handled with a pencil and carefully placed inside a zip-lock bag.

Johnson approached Moroski and Colvin, immediately getting down to business. He didn't care for either man because both were racist pigs. He knew the day would come when he'd be forced to put them in check, but also knew that their bond was stronger than most brothers. If he went up against one, he'd have to deal with both. Today Moroski did the talking while Colvin stood as if ready for battle. Protocol required that he discuss the case with Johnson, but in the field he didn't give a damn about rules. He addressed Hernandez.

"Manny, here's what we got: the victim is one Brenda

Lee Perkins, found dead by her brother, who checked on her whereabouts after she failed to call or show for a family function."

"How long has she been dead?" Manny asked.

"The coroner placed the initial time of death sometime Friday evening, but until confirmed it's only speculation."

"Any witnesses?"

"One, an old lady upstairs named Rutherford. She heard noises as if someone were fighting and saw a black male jump the back fence afterwards."

"Any description of the individual?" Johnson interrupted.

"Only that his hair was in cornrows," Moroski stated to Hernandez, ignoring Johnson.

"Anything else?" Hernandez inquired.

"Just this — the victim's boyfriend was one Earl Robinson, gunned down the other night at the mall shootout. This killing appears to be related."

Hernandez thanked Moroski and Colvin for their assistance then trailed his partner out the door. He knew there was serious tension between those three but couldn't do anything about it. Besides, those two white men didn't like him either, considering him the lesser of two evils. Johnson used every ounce of energy to restrain his emotions.

"What's our next move, Nate?" Manny asked while jotting down notes.

"Jones first, then Henderson," Johnson boomed.

They got inside their vehicle, ignoring the media, and headed for the west side to give Buckey a surprise visit.

Each man was sure that Buckey was the mysterious killer, along with Slack. Past experience led them to believe that Slack would cover his tracks. Still, they would deal with him eventually. Right now Jones was sticking out like a sore thumb.

After parking in front of the house, they trekked up the walkway and forcefully pounded on the door. Buckey and Violet were in the kitchen preparing for their bar-b-que. They had slept late and never started their parties until early evening anyway. The loud knocking on the door brought them both to the foyer.

"This is the police, open up!" Johnson demanded.

"What do you want?" Violet shouted.

"Ma'am, open up the door, we want to talk to Jones."

"He don't want to talk to you."

To Violet's surprise Buckey opened the door, allowing the cops to enter. A smile creased his face from ear to ear, but Johnson found nothing amusing. He along with Hernandez would both remain standing during this entire visit. Buckey and Johnson conversed while Violet watched and Manny flipped open his notepad.

"What can I do for you gentlemen? Would you like some coffee?"

"Look, Jones, we'd like you to answer a few questions."

"Have I committed a crime, sir?"

"Do you know Brenda Perkins?"

"Can't say I do." Buckey calmly stroked his goatee.

"Do you know Earl Robinson?"

"Yes sir, he's a friend of mine. I hated to hear of his murder. Have you found the killer yet?"

"Where were you Friday evening?"

"Officer, I don't know what you're after, but Friday evening I was home with my baby." He smiled while touching Violet's butt.

"Listen, punk, we came here that night and you were gone."

"I'm not your punk and for your information, when you came here I had just left to make a beer run — next question."

"You seem to think this is a joke!" Hernandez roared.

"The only joke is you coming to my home looking for a needle in a haystack when you should be out there chasing the bad guys."

Violet was both surprised and shocked by Buckey's cool demeanor and proper use of language. He didn't have a worry in the world. The fact that he was getting to the man verbally made her proud to be his woman.

"Look, officer, if you're not here to arrest me then I'll have to ask you to leave my home."

"Alright, Jones, but just remember, we will be watching."

"You can watch all you want but won't see a thing. Now if you'll excuse me, I do have some meat to prepare."

Johnson and Hernandez walked out furious, wanting nothing more than to nail that creep to the wall. Somehow they needed to tie him to any of the murders committed, but with nothing concrete Buckey remained a free man. Next the detectives drove to Slack's house, but Buckey's call got there first.

They rolled up to the court then lumbered up the stair-

well to Slack's door. He was on the patio pouring char-
coal into his pit while Yolanda whipped up potato salad,
baked beans, and seasoned meat in the kitchen. Spotting
them from the window, she dried her hands on an apron
and waited at the door.

"Well, if it ain't my old friends Fric n Frac," she growled.

"Thanks for the warm welcome," Hernandez said sarcastically.

"What y'all want?"

"We'd like to speak with your husband."

"Slack, baby, the Keystone Kops are here for you!" she
yelled.

Slack appeared at the door without a care in the world.
The detectives figured that Buckey had probably warned
him that they were on the prowl. Yolanda stood with arms
folded and a menacing stare on her face. Johnson spoke
while Hernandez pulled out his trusty pen and pad.

"Henderson, we want to ask you a few questions."

"What kind of questions?"

"We're investigating some murders and think you
might have some answers."

"Man, I ain't got shit," he said while taking a swig of
wine.

"It tastes better in a glass," Johnson stated.

"Look, dude. . . ."

"That's Sargeant Johnson."

"I really don't give a damn what yo goddamn name is
cause if you ain't here to charge me with a crime then get
the hell out my house."

"Okay, Mister Personality, you've been fingered as the"

triggerman in Ricky Jordan's murder, so either you answer our questions here or downtown — it's your choice."

All Slack heard was that he'd been pointed out as the triggerman. He was furious that someone would have the nerve to tell on him. Whoever it was would surely die, of this he was certain. He spoke in a low chilling tone that was barely audible: "I ain't did nothin and got nothin to say, so if you ain't got an arrest warrant, our conversation is over."

Slack returned to the patio as Johnson and Hernandez stood dumbfounded for a moment then turned to leave. Johnson knew he had pushed the wrong button by mentioning a witness. Hernandez knew it too but didn't care, thinking that if Slack found out the culprit was Eddie Turner, then that would be one less hoodlum on the streets. And if he made a mistake, that would be two. They walked out and returned to their car.

"Nate, I think we need to put a tail on him."

"We will Manny, plus put one on Turner."

"You think he'll figure it out?"

"Yes, I do."

"What's our next move, partner?"

"Let's go back to the station and I'll get the ballistics report on that gun found at the girl's house while you set up the tails on Turner and Henderson."

They returned to headquarters, with Johnson going to the crime lab and Hernandez the chief's office. Meeting at their own office, Hernandez was surprised to see a smile on his partner's usually serious face.

"Good news?" Manny asked.

"Better than that — some skin dug up under Brenda's fingernail belongs to none other than Jones. Also, the DNA tested from the semen in her vagina matches that creep too. We got the bastard signed, sealed, and delivered."

"Let's go," Manny said with flames in his eyes.

They rushed down the hall and out the door with urgency. Johnson had flashing red lights spinning wildly on the dash as Manny radioed for backup. Arriving at Buckey's crib in two minutes flat, Johnson ran to the front door while his partner made his way around back. Buckey heard tires screeching along with the sirens and bolted for the back door. Violet opened the front, staring daggers at Johnson.

"Man, what the fuck you beatin on my door like that for?"

"Listen, lady, we . . ."

Before Johnson had time to complete his sentence, he and Violet heard commotion coming from the back yard. Violet attempted to stop him from entering, but Johnson tossed her to the side and ran through the kitchen. As he reached the door, all he got was a glimpse of Buckey scaling the fence. When he looked out he saw Hernandez sprawled on the ground bloody and unconscious. The brick Buckey used lay innocently next to Manny's body. Johnson rushed through the home ordering Violet not to leave, then hurried to the car and radioed for more assistance.

"Officer down, officer down, we need assistance. Suspect is Curtis 'Buckey' Jones, black male, twenty-eight, five nine, one eighty, cornrow braids, tattoos, mustache, goatee, armed and dangerous, last seen in the vicinity of

Tenth and Chestnut, possibly headed for the Acorn housing complex."

Cops throughout the city converged on the Acorn because when someone messed with one of their own, he was as good as nailed. In the next two hours not a home or yard would go unchecked if five-o deemed it necessary.

Buckey saw Johnson hit the corner and sprinted through the complex, exiting on Eighth. Shooting through Da Mo'houses and across Seventh, he ran to an industrial area, taking back paths that only neighborhood residents knew existed. Winding up at the *Tribune's* service yard on 3rd, he hopped into a company truck, pulled a dirty cap low on his head, and sped away. His mind raced wildly, but he vowed that if he was going down, it wouldn't be alone.

Johnson noticed a newspaper truck doing ninety while headed up the ramp onto 880 and correctly assumed it was Buckey. Putting the pedal to the metal, he gave chase. The delivery truck was no match for the police car, but Buckey tried to outrun it anyway. He sideswiped cars, creating tailspins and a massive traffic jam.

With the Highway Patrol joining the chase, Buckey laughed and drove even crazier. Exiting at High Street, he shot into the Super K parking lot. Noticing an elderly couple about to enter their car, he jacked them. The gentleman resisted, and that mistake cost him his life. Buckey pulled his piece, shooting him dead while his wife screamed in horror. She was petrified, praying he would not kill her too.

Buckey shoved the woman inside the car then hauled

ass without regard for traffic signals. Hitting 880 in the opposite direction, he headed right back to the only thing he knew, the west side. Unknown to him, police had halted traffic in both directions, so the freeway was empty.

Helicopters hovered above with squad cars cautiously trailing. Spectators gawked at each overpass as the car zoomed down the highway. Five-o had set up a roadblock at Fifth Avenue but Buckey drove right through it. Officers opened a lane when it became apparent he would not yield. In similar circumstances they would have blown him to hell, but since he had taken a hostage they couldn't shoot.

With the car moving at a snail's pace, he pressed the muzzle of the gun to the woman's heart. Sharpshooters positioned themselves to take him out, but their orders were to hold their fire. No one wanted to be held accountable for the lady dying. If someone shot and missed, it was almost certain that would trigger this fool to kill his hostage. If they struck him, the chain reaction could even cause him to pull the trigger involuntarily.

Within minutes, every major television network interrupted its regular programming to plaster Buckey's mug shot on the screen. They knew he had killed the husband of the woman being held hostage. The media also now had the facts on Brenda's murder, and even though Buckey had not been tried in a court of law, by the time regular programming was returned, no jury in the county would acquit this maniac.

Once he passed the roadblock, Buckey accelerated, with five-o chasing in hot pursuit. He took the 980 interchange and shot up the 17th Street exit. When he attempted to make a left turn on 17th, which was a one-way street with traffic going the opposite direction, the car spun out of control. It hopped the curb and careened into a pump at a self-serve gas station.

Gas sprouted up like a gusher as people at the station ran like mad. Buckey pushed the woman out the passenger side, diving out right behind her. Violently he grabbed her by the throat with the gun pressed to her temple. The sharpshooters were in position and ready to take him out when the pump exploded into a towering inferno.

Thick black smoke clouded the sky, with flames shooting thirty feet in the air. This was just the diversion Buckey needed. Tossing the lady aside like a rag doll, he looked for an escape route, spotting an elderly black man hanging up the pay phone. Buckey put the gun to his neck, forced him into his van, then slid in behind him. Next he ordered the gentleman to drive down 18th to the west side.

Crouching down, Buckey smiled as they drove to safety. When they got to the corner of 18th and Market, he ordered the man out then sped away in the vehicle. The old guy stood there shaking in his boots but happy to be alive. Abandoning the van at McClymond's High, Buckey got out and briskly walked away. Taking side streets, he headed for the one place where he knew he would be safe.

22
GETTING EVEN

Slack went into his usual shell the minute Fric n Frac walked out. Yolanda knew he would kill today, so she finished cooking the meat while he oiled up one of his guns. It would be a waste of time asking where he was going or who was the victim, so she stayed out of his way. He walked out of the bedroom, kissed her on the cheek, and told her, "I'll be back; don't wait up."

She was always a nervous wreck when her man had killing on his mind, but for some reason today she was not. She'd heard it from The Man herself, so she knew someone had to pay. There was no doubt that Slack would be there to collect. He was dressed in a light blue sweatsuit with matching tennis shoes and golf cap. Jumping into his beat-up hooptie, he cut out.

DeFermery Park was packed with people celebrating Independence Day. Situated in the heart of the west side, it is outlined by 16th, 18th, Adeline, and Union streets. The entire park covers six square city blocks, so it is huge. Its recreation center has the appearance of an old plantation house complete with front sitting porch. The building is situated fifty feet from the street and is surrounded by plush green grass, cobblestone walkways, and a drive-in parking lot.

Behind the parking area are tennis courts which always have to be swept clean of broken bottles and trash. Next to the courts are the sand box and playground. Once upon a time there were tether-ball poles and hopscotch markings, but now all that remains is asphalt along with hoop courts without nets. To the left is the bar-b-que and picnic area, if you can call it that. You have to create your own picnic spot and most of the time bring your own pit, too.

Today, as usual, there were some picnic tables occupied by old men playing dominoes. The OGs would be there at the crack of dawn, plying their trade with the stakes high. The best domino games happened at DeFermery, just like Wino Park had craps, and if you weren't a true player, then you would be wise not to come.

Two-man teams with the game going to two hundred were the order of the day, along with no talking by the players. The skill level was so tight that if a partner was playing to his partner's hand, he would in the most subtle of maneuvers slam his bone down on the wood. This gesture let his accomplice know to keep playing that particular style.

At the rear of the park was a baseball diamond used for

Little League players. It wasn't large enough for teenage or high school play, but for the kids it was fine. An after-school checkout room sat to the right of the diamond where kids checked out bats, balls, or tennis rackets, using only a shirt or jacket for collateral. The used-to-be high school stars or drunks would check a b-ball from time to time and participate in horrible games, attempting to relive their past.

The restrooms were connected to the checkout room and could best be described as pitiful. Dealing, sex for money, plus drug use happened continuously throughout the day. Outside the restrooms sat a metal ping pong table painted green with a metal divider in place of a net. Next to that were practice areas for tennis players to work on their game. The swimming pool was beautiful, but unlike public facilities in certain parts of the city (white neighborhoods in general), this pool was only open during summer months. As usual, the predominantly black neighborhood got the short end of the stick.

Slack pulled into the parking lot of the multi-service center located across the street from the park. The center houses the west-side branch library, a daily lunch program for seniors, mental health outreach, and job placement program.

Walking over to the park, Slack made his way to the restroom where he would wait, because he knew as sure as the sun was shining that his victim sooner or later would come to him. It happened sooner.

Eddie Turner was having a helluva day, hustling three-card monte on buses for a few hours and making a killing.

In the process he'd picked up a floozie named Cheryl who was tight with curves in all the right places. She followed him to his family get-together because she liked his game.

Eddie was five ten, one eighty, and caramel-colored handsome. A sharp dresser, he was decked out in a gold Italian two-piece suit with matching brim, socks, and shoes. A multi-colored rayon shirt accented his attire. Drinking beers one after the next, he felt good about his hustle, bank, and the thought of screwing Cheryl. Excusing himself, he headed for the restroom to pay his water bill.

Stepping up to the urinal, he unzipped his fly and allowed his stream to flow. Some fool was in a stall, but Eddie paid little attention, thinking the clown had a little dick and was afraid someone would know his secret. One thing Turner was extremely proud of was his manhood.

The dude passed behind him, then the door closed. He looked up and saw Slack standing with a 357 Magnum aimed at his head with a silencer on the tip. Before he could say a word he was dead, shit pouring from his body and ruining the suit. Blood splattered the walls as brain matter coated the floor.

Slack walked out and placed a padlock on the door. Putting on dark mirror sunglasses and pulling his golf cap down to his eyebrows, he hit a beeline to his ride. Wiping the gun free of prints, he tossed it in the center's dumpster after removing the silencer. His normal modus operandi would be to throw away any incriminating evidence, but silencers were hard to come by, so he kept it. He got home and opened a fresh bottle of wine, kissed

Yolanda on the lips, and told everyone in the house, "The party's on."

Yolanda was the happiest person in the room because she knew they didn't have anything else to worry about. The eyewitness couldn't talk, so Fric n Frac had no case. She would drop the bomb on his skinny ass tonight, of that she was sure.

23
A WOMAN
SCORNED

Police were crawling through the house like ants when all of a sudden the television caught everyone's attention. Buckey's horse-looking mug was front and center as the anchorman relayed details to the viewers. The commanding officer gave instructions to cops on where to go in case Buckey took one of the downtown turnoffs.

Violet was as worried as worry could get knowing that her man was Oaktown's Most Wanted. The newscaster was giving a chronological description of Buckey's shenanigans when Violet became paralyzed in her seat.

The words were like atomic bombs exploding inside her head, long after regular programming returned. She didn't want to believe it, but they repeated it so much she knew it had to be true. If it wasn't true, she reasoned, then why did he run? As long as she lived, she would never forget these words:

"POLICE ALSO TESTED SEMEN FROM MISS PERKINS' BODY, FINDING IT TO BE A DNA MATCH TO JONES."

Violet's heart sank because she loved Buckey with every fiber of her being. To know he'd been blessing another woman behind her back turned her world upside down. The house was total chaos, with officers running to their cars and scurrying about, but Violet remained seated with her hands gripping her head.

Finally she got up, casually went upstairs to put on a coat, then walked out the front door. Her mind was in a fog, but she located the car in the Acorn lot then drove slowly down Adeline. Arriving at her destination, she failed to remember how she got there.

Spodie's mother was staying with relatives, so Buckey figured that would be the last place The Man would look for anything. That was the reason he had stashed his dope and loot in Spodie's garage, thinking that the pigs had no reason to return to a crime scene that had been turned inside out.

It was the perfect hiding spot that only he, Violet, and Slack knew about. Arriving late at night he had hidden his property wrapped in foil inside the air filter of an old Chevy. Buckey had all senses on alert, but when he peeped out the window he dropped his guard. Violet entered, and when Buckey hugged her tightly he failed to notice that her body did not respond. She stood rigid as a board with her mind in a fog.

"Ah'm glad you came, baby — ah didn't know how we was gone hook up. What we hafta do is make a plan. First..."

"Why you fuck her?"

"Fuck who, Vi?"

"Niggah, don't play me cheap, you know damn well who."

"Baby, wait a minute, I'ont know who tole you dat lie but..."

Violet pulled the gun from behind her back, aiming at Buckey's heart. She didn't care anymore.

"Baby, put da gun down," he pleaded while whipping out a pistol of his own.

"I gave you everything I had, but it wasn't enough."

"Violet, put down da gun."

"Lie for you, cheat, steal, kill ...."

"Bitch, ah'm only gone say dis one moe time — put da muthafuckin gun down and let's talk dis shit..."

The first shot struck his rib cage, causing Buckey to stumble backwards.

"Baby, why you do dat?"

She answered by firing another bullet, which lodged in his chest. Blood poured from his mouth and his eyes grew large as bo-dollars when he saw her pointing the gun barrel at his eyeballs. They fired simultaneously, with her bullet digging a tunnel through his nose and exiting the back of his head, causing it to split in half. His return shot punctured one of those big breasts he adored, searing it and killing her instantly.

Their bodies were found a few hours later by five-o tracing the car, which was registered to Violet. The cops labeled it a murder/suicide to ease the public's mind. Hernandez became an instant hero, earning the Medal of Valor, which was the highest award the rollers bestowed on an officer.

Johnson could not understand how his partner got the damn award when all he did was get his ass whipped. Still, he was happy the killings were over. The community could now breathe a sigh of relief.

24
Rest in Peace

Cassandra woke before I did and had breakfast prepared and the table set. Stretching while turning over, I inhaled the sweet aroma of coffee percolating. Feeling the morning paper next to my body, I opened it then yelled for Cassandra to come in the room. Showing her the headlines, I read aloud the article describing the gruesome details of Buckey and Violet.

When we finished, I told her about the phone call last night threatening my life, but she assured me that the only thing getting killed would be the demons inside Buckey's body. After showering together we ate, got dressed, and went to Pearlie Mae's house.

The limo arrived on schedule, then Charles led the family in prayer. As we cruised to the funeral home, I said a silent prayer along with giving thanks to the Lord because finally my brother would rest in peace.

It Ain't Over

The Fourth was a scorcher, but the prison allowed the inmates extra time for recreation along with a decent meal of ribs, baked beans, potato salad, and corn on the cob. While everyone was watching baseball, the program was interrupted for a special news bulletin.

There plastered on the screen was Buckey's mug, with the anchorman giving vivid descriptions of the murders committed during the week. They blamed everything on him, and five-o was in hot pursuit.

Watching the chase intently, Shakey was proud to see baby bro elude the dragnet. The inmates cheered once it became apparent he had escaped. Later that night Shakey called Nadine collect to find out more. That was when she told him that Buckey and Violet were dead.

The details were sketchy, but she did say that Rainbow and Cassandra had given the rollers information on

Buckey. Enraged, he had Nadine put him on hold then call that fool's house on her three-way. She'd obtained the number from someone at Rainbow's job by posing as a family friend mourning Stoney's death. Shakey instructed her not to crack a peep.

"Hello."

"Rainbow?" His voice was low and chilling.

"Yeah, who is this?"

"Don't matter."

"What you want, Don't Matter?"

"You a dead man."

He slammed down the phone and returned to his cell, not bothering to call Nadine back. Rainbow would be in for a big surprise very soon. The fact that he had a smart mouth only increased Shakey's anger. The three-month wait would seem like an eternity.

Questions or comments, email Renay:
LADAYPUBLISHING@CS.COM

Thanks for your support!!

ABOUT THE AUTHOR

Renay Jackson is a former rapper and street lit author with five novels to his credit, all of which will be published by Frog, Ltd. over a two-year period. Jackson received the Chester Himes Black Mystery Writer Award in 2002. A single father to three daughters and a niece, he lives in Oakland, California, where he has been a custodian for the Oakland Police Department for more than fifteen years.